I0627381

Grey Angel

A Queendom Tale

Dani Finn

Content warnings

This book is intended for **adult audiences** and contains violence, cursing, and explicit sex, including scenes between humans and <redacted>.

ONE

Ynis wiped her blade on the fallen geller's back. Convenient of them to have a stripe of such fine hair along their spines and across their shoulders; it made cleaning her sword after killing one that much easier. It was so soft and sleek, mud-puddle brown in contrast to the mottled greenish-grey skin on most of its body. Despite the color, its bloodied face, in profile, looked almost human, if she ignored the fangs poking between its chapped lips.

She glanced around at her companions, whose easy posture showed there were no more live geller in the area. She pulled off a glove, tucking it into her belt so it wouldn't get dirty, and ran her fingers through the unsullied part of its fur near the back of its neck. It was even softer than it looked, with a texture finer than any beast of her ken. She supposed it offered some protection for its spine, but she couldn't figure out the natural logic behind it. Why have fur there and not elsewhere? Maybe it was as some said, that geller weren't natural at all, but spawned from nether portals, invaders from an eldritch world.

Though they were ferocious in close combat, they weren't very organized, posing limited challenge for groups of trained, armored Haemene. Ynis' squad was the best in the castle and had never suffered a casualty at these beasts' claws. But what the geller lacked in discipline, they made up for in unpredictability. Groups would appear, seemingly out of nowhere, and kill anything they came across, animal or human. If these had made it to the settlements outside of Dall, they would have met with little resistance. Entire households could have been slaughtered. Where had they come from? And why all at once, when geller hadn't been seen here for more than a decade?

"A small group has escaped—" Guin stopped to salute as Ynis rose. Ynis nodded for them to continue. "Yul and Poddeh are tracking them with the dogs. We'll have them rounded up before nightfall."

"Casualties?"

Guin shook their head. "Couple bruises, but nothing to speak of." They glanced down at Ynis' ungloved hand, frowning. "You touched it with your bare hand?" Geller were thought to carry diseases, but over the past few months, Ynis had gotten their blood on her skin countless times, and in her eyes and mouth more than once, and had suffered no ill effects.

"It has the softest fur. I should make a coat of it. With sharp shoulders and wide lapels, and long, down to about here." Ynis chopped with her hand mid-calf, picturing herself walking in the wind, fur fluttering across her body in waves.

"If that's what you want." Guin pulled out a long knife and knelt by the fallen geller. "It'll take a dozen of them, I should think, but this will be a start." They pulled the fur taut on the back of its head and lined up their knife.

"Wait." Ynis suddenly felt a little queasy at the thought of wearing these beasts as a coat. "It's too much, isn't it."

Guin swiveled, knife still in hand, squinting up at her. "Fashion's not my strong suit, I'm afraid."

"Let's deal with the stragglers and I'll mull it over." She loved the fact that Guin was ready to start skinning geller on the spot, no questions asked, but it would be ugly, bloody work, and she didn't particularly want to hear those wet ripping sounds just now.

"As you say, Mena." They gave another salute, which Ynis waved off, and spun away to consult with Jarris and Kegh. Ynis hated the formal title, but Guin was old-fashioned like that. When they were in armor, military rules applied, no exceptions. She scanned the field, counting four dead geller, two of which she'd accounted for herself. This would be a mixed group, two, maybe three bands who'd roam together and wreak havoc for a while until the Haemene caught up with them or they turned on each other and cut their own number in half.

Bigger groups were easier to deal with. The Watch could spot one from the air with their falcons and have a squad sent out within hours. It was the lone geller you had to worry about, ones that got pushed out by their group, or split off for whatever reason. They tended to be wilier, staying out of sight and choosing their targets more carefully. Gods knew how many of them roamed the foothills.

The barking of the dogs in the distance signaled that the remaining geller had been found. Ynis sheathed her sword and followed the others, running toward the sound. Chances were, the geller would already be dead by the time she arrived, but she was the mena, and she would not leave anything to chance.

The keening wail of a geller pierced the dusk, ending suddenly, no doubt felled by a blade. The dogs' barking turned to feral growling. As she rounded a boulder, she saw them tearing at the neck and face of a geller whose limbs spasmed, then twitched and went still. Another lay dead at Poddeh's feet. A third one crouched atop a boulder, hissing and spitting at the Haemene now surrounding it, who jumped back to avoid its foul saliva. Ynis studied the boulder for a moment; it would be a difficult climb, giving the geller's claws a chance to inflict damage or knock her off.

Guin held up their crossbow almost apologetically. Haemene were forbidden from using such weapons except in exigent circumstances. Though geller hardly qualified as worthy adversaries, she hated the idea of bringing death to a defenseless opponent.

"Mena?" Guin glanced from the geller back to Ynis.

"Shoot it."

Guin raised the bow and sighted. The geller bared its saliva-frothed teeth, yellow eyes burning with rage. It fell without a sound, the bolt sticking out of its eye socket.

"That's all of them," Yul said, shooing the dogs off the mangled corpse. The other lay on the ground, its arm neatly hacked off at the shoulder, dead eyes and mouth open to the sky. Ynis turned away, suddenly queasy at the sight of the carnage, even of beasts such as this. She'd seen worse in the spice wars, fields soaked in blood, carrion birds pecking at dying soldiers, gore crusting her gloves stiff. Why was this hitting her harder?

Soft footsteps approached. Guin.

"The...pelts?" they asked quietly. Ynis shook her head without turning around.

"Pile the beasts and burn them." She pulled out a soft cloth and began wiping the sticky blood from her armor. A long night of cleaning and polishing lay ahead.

As they mounted their horses and turned away from the stinking bonfire, something tugged at the back of Ynis' mind. She turned her horse sideways, scanning the horizon; there was nothing to be seen in the growing dusk. Her instincts told her she'd missed something, but the rest of the group had already started riding. She scanned the darkness once more and followed, trailed by the unshakable suspicion that she was being watched.

Guin matched Ynis' silence in the muck room while helping remove Ynis' armor and placing the pieces on the table for cleaning. The others were jovial, recounting their kills and teasing each other with the warmth of victorious warriors. The room filled with good-natured laughter as they hung up their armor and weapons after far too little cleaning. Ynis nodded thanks to Guin, then set about wiping down her armor with lavender-scented oil. One of the dragons on her breastplate had a scratch on it from a geller's claws that she couldn't buff out. She'd have to have the armorer refinish it for her. The others soon trundled out, laughing more quietly now, off to feast and drink their fill, as befitted the occasion. Ynis wanted nothing more than a hot bath to scald the grime from her body and the memories from her mind.

Guin hung their hauberk in their cubby, then wiped their hands on a rag. "If there's nothing else?"

Ynis gestured lazily toward the door. "Go. Eat, drink. Be merry."

Guin bit their lip, eyes dark with worry, then nodded and disappeared.

Back in her room, Ynis pumped hot water into the tub. She tossed a handful of rose-scented soap in, then slipped into the scalding water. She ran through each kill in her mind as she scrubbed every inch of her skin, making mental notes of a poor angle of attack in one case and the slip of her boot on the gritty sand in another. Neither had proved costly. It was nearly impossible for a geller's claws to pierce her armor, but this review was part of her process. It was her duty to be better than everyone else, to give them something to strive for.

She lathered her hair, which had spent the better part of the day crammed into her sweaty helmet, and leaned back until only her face protruded from the water. She should probably drain the bath and run it again to get properly clean, but it would already take an eternity to dry her hair before bed as it was. Clean enough would have to do. She could always bathe again in the morning.

She dried herself off and wrapped a towel around her head to begin the process, wondering if Guin was drinking with the others or if they'd gone off to the shrine to do their rituals. Ynis hated religion as a rule, but Guin's practice seemed harmless enough. If preparing their mind for the visit of some mythical Grey Angel kept them steady in the face of the geller threat, who was Ynis to object?

Sleep was elusive, and of course she got hungry after the kitchen was closed and had to resort to gnawing on some jerky she found in her travel kit. It was sufficient but deeply unsatisfying. Not unlike the day's sortie. Hunting down and killing a pack of geller with no casualties was a good thing, but it felt like trying to empty the Fulli River with a thimble. As she brushed out her hair, which was almost dry by the time the midnight chime sounded, her mind drifted back to the feeling she'd had as they rode off.

Her instincts had told her someone was watching. Her instincts were seldom wrong.

Two

Guin lay in their bunk, arms crossed over their chest. Only Poddeh still rustled in their sheets; Jarris and Kegh were snoring already. The midnight chime had sounded, and all was still, or still enough. All Guin could do was keep their mind open and wait.

They batted away thoughts of how presumptuous it was to hope that the Grey Angel would pick them out of the untold thousands of practitioners scattered through-out the Queendom. And the Kingdom, though most had emigrated after the Cleavage. Many practiced their whole lives, never to be graced by Her shadowy presence. What chance did a neophyte like Guin have? They deepened their breathing, exhaling these intrusive thoughts, shed-ding them like ripples away from a thrown pebble, until the center was clear again.

They summoned the image as easily as blinking. Her stony face was bathed in shadow, tendrils of black hair floating in the air. Wings like a night eagle, ashen grey and sleek in the moonlight, spread wide before folding neatly onto Her back. Her lips alone bore color, mauve blending toward delicate pink when they stretched into the faintest smile. Her dark eyes fixed Guin with a knowing look. The Grey Angel could see the truth people hid from themselves and reveal it to them if She deemed them worthy. It was even said She could grant wishes.

What would Guin ask for if She blessed them with a visit?

Guin maintained three ready options, as recommended by their Teacher. They tended to shift over time; the things they'd wished for as a teenager seemed foolish now that they were in their twenties. This night, they wished for wisdom, the ability to see through their own emotions to assess each decision objectively, with care and caution. Last night, it had been endurance, after a long, hard run in the rain, though it always felt cheap wishing for something physical. Before that, the ability to quickly learn languages. Guilt bubbled up as their secret Fourth Desire lurked just below the surface. Guin clenched their teeth, then forced their jaw to relax. They would not allow that to cloud their mind this night.

They did another breath cycle, pushing their thoughts to the side and centering the vision. The Angel's eyes burned like black suns. Guin strove to open themself to Her darkness, to bathe in the shadows She cast. She knew things about Guin that they hid from themself, things She might tell them if they stared deeply enough into the healing void of Her eyes.

First Hour came and went without a visit as always. Guin blinked away the vision, and the contours of the dark room came into focus in the faint starlight. Poddeh had stopped moving and joined the chorus of soft snores. All was still in the castle. Guin took in a deep breath and tried to let their disappointment out with it. Each night offered new hope, and every day an opportunity to make themself worthy.

"Poddeh, you'll go with Yul to search the knobs. Jerris and Kegh will take the river bluffs. Guin, you and I will comb the Greenhills."

Guin touched their chest in disbelief—surely Poddeh or Yul would be better suited to accompany the mena. Any of them, really; Guin was always spotted at least a point in duels and seldom won. Ynis' firm clap on their shoulder startled them back to the moment.

"Everyone, get your gear together and meet me at the front gate by fourth bell. You'll be gone for three days, so pack accordingly." Ynis spoke with gentle authority, demanding attention without raising her voice. Her tone shifted lower as she continued. "We'll be hunting geller, in packs of up to four, according to the Watch falcons. You are authorized to use missile weapons in this hunt, should you choose." Guin had never seen Ynis use one, so they would have to be prepared. "Kitchen is prepping the meal kits now. Any questions?" Everyone looked at each other for an awkward moment. "Off you go then." The others nodded and departed. Ynis returned Guin's salute with annoyance. "Enough with the formality. As your mena, I command you not to salute me."

"Mena," Guin acknowledged with a nod.

"And stop calling me that. My name is—"

"Ynis. It won't happen again."

Ynis ran a hand down her face, but she was smiling. "We'll be traveling together for three days or more. There's no time to stand on ceremony. Titles and salutes and the like..." She waved them away with a frown. "They're a vestige from before we split from the Kingdom. The Haemene continued those traditions, but they don't mesh well with the First Principles, do they? I've often thought—" She shook her head. "Just talk to me like you would any other member of the Haemene. Just for this trip. As a personal favor to me." She touched her chest, then poked Guin's gently, sparking a confusing mix of heat and annoyance. "And to yourself."

Guin forced a smile, which became a real one when Ynis returned it. They looked down, embarrassment burning in their cheeks. "I'll see what I can do," they managed, peeking back up to see Ynis scanning her notepad. "I'll just go get my things together, then."

"You do that. I'll pick up the meal kits and meet you back here a little before fourth?"

Guin nodded, confused as to why the mena—Ynis, they corrected themself—wouldn't just ask them to get the food. Surely, she had more important things to do. Maybe it was a First Principles thing. *Do for others when you can; accept from others when you must.* The phrase stuck in their head as they checked the contents of their pack and filled their waterskin. As a child, they'd always fancied the "take from others when you must" part as permission to steal in times of need, despite the explicit teachings to the contrary. Wasn't it okay to steal in order to survive? Surely a stranger's comfort didn't outweigh your life or death. They'd never said it out loud, but they wondered sometimes.

They strapped their crossbow to their pack and secured their broadsword and main-gauche to their belt. Some Haemene carried shields, while a few like Ynis wielded greatswords, but Guin preferred to be more mobile. They slid the throwing daggers into the back of each boot, checked their laces, and glanced around their mostly empty cubby. Everything was in its place. Fourth bell was not far off.

They returned to the courtyard to find Ynis already standing tall and proud, armor glinting in the morning sun, dark hair braided into a single long plait running down her back. She was talking to a pair of young girls who looked up at her, starstruck. Not for the first time, Guin mused that Ynis would make an amazing mother. Though as a Shaped woman, she wouldn't be able to become one in the usual way. Was that hard for her? If it was, she never let it show.

"...join the Haemene when I'm grown," one of the girls was saying.

"I'm sure you will," Ynis said warmly, touching the bright-eyed girl on the shoulder, "if you work every day like the Queendom depends on it. Because one day, it might." She winked at Guin, stirring a sense of pride mixed with self-doubt. "Speaking of which..." She greeted Guin with a formal salute, no doubt to remind the girls of the seriousness of the endeavor.

"Thank you, Mena," the girls said, offering little salutes to her and to Guin before scurrying off, giggling.

Ynis watched them leave with a fond smile on her face, which lingered as she turned to Guin. "Fine weather for hunting." She closed her eyes and breathed in deeply through her nose. Guin treasured such brief moments, when they could look upon her face and not feel the weight of her regard, the fear of not measuring up. Of not being worthy.

"We might see rain in a few days." Guin regretted the words as soon as they came out. Why put a damper on Ynis' mood?

"It's easier tracking in the mud anyway. Come, let's head down to the gate and meet the others."

Guin walked behind Ynis by instinct; she was their mena, after all, however much she hated the title. But Ynis kept slowing down and turning to talk to them, so Guin gave up and walked alongside her through the cobbled alley leading down to the gate.

"The morning report tells of a cow torn apart just outside of Dall and a shepherd gone missing not far from there." Ynis spoke as if these were opportunities for valor.

"You think it's geller?"

Ynis gave a single nod. "Not a group, I don't think, or not a very large one. None have been spotted, but there aren't many wolves left in the Greenhills, and bear haven't been seen there in decades." She held out a hand, as if presenting evidence. "I don't see what else it could be."

Guin grunted agreement. Solo geller were thought to hide during the day and only attack at night. As a result, they were notoriously hard to catch.

They fetched their horses and met the others by the main gate. Ynis gave one of her curt speeches, reviewing instructions and emphasizing safety. "The Haemene guard those who love the Queen, which we can't do if we're dead. Dismissed."

Ynis rode out first at a fast trot. Guin had to push her horse to catch up, which wasn't an ideal way to start a potentially long trip. Ynis had told them to pack for three days, but everyone knew that meant six. So, they either hunted or begged for food, or they went hungry for the other three.

Tradition held that any house should provide a roof and a meal to any Haemene who requested it, but not everyone was equally enthusiastic about the Haemene's mission. In fairness, there had been isolated cases of abuse of privilege, but nothing as bad as the King's Guard back in the Kingdom. No one was under any obligation to like the Haemene, but most were friendly enough, or they kept their animosity to themselves. In any case, it didn't affect Guin's desire to protect them.

They followed Bottoms Road, which was muddy in spots but not swamped like it had been in spring. They stopped briefly at each puddle and muddy patch but saw nothing more than hoof and boot prints, plus the occasional marks of a deer or small mammal. Nothing like the distinctive pairs of clawed tracks of the geller, one set deeper than the other. Geller stood on their hind legs to fight or climb, but they used all four to run faster than any human.

Ynis didn't speak much, which suited Guin just fine. They never knew how to *be* around her. She said she wanted to be treated like a fellow Haemene, but she was so sure of herself, always so in command. It was hard to see her as anything but their leader. It was also hard to see her and not feel a twinge of...jealousy? Regret? She made everything look so easy.

"We'll branch off on some game trails once we pass Feyan's Bog." Ynis gestured toward the hill rising above the conifers of the bog. A forest of leafy green stretched into the distance, with only a few splashes of yellow hinting at the coming season. "And at some point, we might need to leave the horses for stealth, but..." She sucked her teeth lightly. "I don't love the idea of leaving them tied up with geller afoot."

Guin lifted a finger, then dropped it hastily. Ynis caught their eye, brow arched inquisitively. Guin looked down, shaking their head.

"Spit it out." Ynis held out her gauntleted hand as if to catch Guin's words.

Guin sighed. "I don't even think it's a good idea, but...supposing we found evidence of geller activity in an area, and we could find the right setup—"

Ynis' armor jingled a little as she clapped her hands together. "We'll use them as bait!"

Guin instinctively rubbed their horse's ears. Wings of Night had carried them safely through dozens of missions, and sometimes people didn't give horses enough credit for sensing tone. "Only if we're prepared to use our crossbows." Guin's cheeks flushed as they spoke; it was bold of them to dictate strategy to their mena. Far too bold.

"Deal." Ynis stuck out a hand, which Guin took, awkwardly at first, but managing to return Ynis' strength with strength, as befitted a fellow soldier. "Now let's just—"

Ynis stopped cold when a falcon squealed and dove at top speed from the sky, flapping to a halt on her now outstretched arm. Its talons settled into the grooves she had built into her armor and waited patiently as she shucked her other gauntlet. She opened the capsule and retrieved the tiny scroll. She read it with a grim expression, then handed it to Guin.

Geller pack of 4 spotted descending Rough Valley. Proceed at full speed to intercept before sunset.

That was almost twenty miles in half a day, a challenge even for their Valley-bred horses, as loaded as they were.

"Duty calls!" Ynis took the scroll and stamped it with her ring before rolling it up painstakingly—clearly a challenge with one hand—and sliding it back into the capsule. "Off you go!" She clucked her cheek twice, and the bird flapped off into the sky. She sighed and spun her horse around. "And off *we* go."

Guin followed suit without a word. Soon they were flying down Bottoms Road, mud kicked up by their horses' pounding hooves. Guin relished the feel of speed, the horse's eagerness, Ynis' resolve. Travelers on foot and horse, carriage, and cart got out of their way as they thundered past. Guin wished they could have slowed down, shown a little courtesy; the Haemene didn't have the friendliest reputation, even among those who approved of their mission. Ynis had never cared about things like that; there was always only one goal with her, and as a result, she seldom failed. It was part of why Guin admired her so much.

It also made it hard to treat her like a fellow soldier, as Ynis had asked. When she spoke, Guin's mind leapt to attention. Ynis might pretend to treat them as an equal, but Guin knew they were not worthy of such an honor.

They slowed as they approached the bridge over Rough Valley, then stopped a hundred yards short, so Ynis could check her map book. "There's a path down on the other side." She gestured, still staring down at the book, tracing a line with her finger. "We'll tie the horses to that tree and hope we're not too late."

Three

Ynis crept through the ferny underbrush alongside the stream, greatsword in hand. Guin trailed a little behind her, crossbow at the ready, scanning the opposite bank while Ynis stared into the forest's shadowy dark. The rushing of the creek should mute their passage, but the same would be true of the geller. She hoped, being numerous, they might make enough noise to give her a warning before they were in sight. Four on two was fine odds; she could take on four by herself if need be, but with the benefit of surprise, the geller could prove dangerous.

"Psst." Ynis stopped at Guin's call. She turned to see them crouching, hand to their ear. Ynis heard it too, then: crashing brush, the patter of small hooves, the huffing warning call of the fern deer. Ynis ducked behind a tree with a large fern growing in front of it, nodding to Guin, who darted toward the edge of the woods and held their crossbow at the ready. Four of the small deer raced by, darting suddenly right as they passed. They must have seen her, she thought in the half-second before the *chunk* of Guin's crossbow sounded and a snarling yowl rose from the direction of the creek.

Ynis tore off running toward the sound, pausing by Guin, who was hastily reloading their crossbow.

"Two in the forest, two by the creek. Maybe one, now." A pained moan rose ahead, followed by a fierce snarl and the scrabbling of claws on rock. The snap of a twig to her left told her the geller in the forest were approaching with attempted stealth. She gestured Guin toward the creek with her eyes and slow-stepped, crouching, in the direction of the sound. She stopped, holding her breath as she listened, but there was nothing to be heard above the rushing of the creek. The *twang* of Guin's crossbow pierced the air, immediately followed by a brief wail and the sound of a body falling on rock.

Ynis turned her attention back to the forest in time to see a greenish-grey shape launch down at her from above. She took a half step back and timed her swing to cut the beast in two, but was tackled from behind by another, claws scrabbling around her neck and helmet as it rode her face-first into the ground. The weight of the other one landing on her knocked the breath from her lungs. She gasped helplessly as they tore at her armor, dislodging a shoulder plate. She managed a shout as one creature's jaws closed on her trapezius, sending a blast of hot pain through her neck and head. She bucked and threw them off, but they were on her again before she could stand, one wrapped around her torso and the other around her legs as her sword lay useless on the ground.

Claws rent the location of the bite, piercing her now-tattered hauberk and spilling warm blood over her neck. She kneed the beast that was on her legs in the face, sending it reeling back, then freed her dagger from her belt and sank it into the neck of the one raking her. It dropped in a mess of hot, stinking blood as the other one rose, teeth bared and eyes glaring. It crouched, then sprang, squealing in the air as Guin's bolt speared its chest. It landed on her with the weight of a dead thing. Guin shouldered their crossbow and drew their sword as they approached, sticking it into each of the dead geller.

"Mena." Guin crouched by Ynis, already pulling out a clean rag to press into her wound. Ynis took the rag from Guin and shooed them back with an angry tilt of her head.

"FUCK!" Ynis shouted, loud enough that every geller within ten miles must have heard. "Mother of backdoor cunt fuckers! FUCK!"

Guin hovered awkwardly, no doubt unsure how to react to this burst of profanity. They shucked their pack and fished out the bottle of antiseptic. "Here, Ynis." Their apologetic tone told her they regretted calling her Mena. But in that moment, it had felt right somehow.

Ynis took the bottle, wincing as the movement caused a hot spike in her shoulder. "Fucking sneaky little..." She turned her head toward the wound, raising the bottle with her good hand but unable to get the rag in place with her injured arm. She ground her teeth, looking up at Guin and holding the bottle toward them.

Guin took it back. "Sorry."

"You don't have to be sorry. I'm the one who—fuuuu-uck," she hissed through clenched teeth as the antiseptic soaked into the wound, which fizzed at the contact. She hated cursing in front of her soldiers, but it helped release some of her anger at being so stupid as to get surprised by two geller. Guin laid a fresh bandage on the wound and held it in place, ignoring Ynis' hand reaching for it.

"Just let me keep pressure on it for a little while."

"It's nothing, I can do it." Ynis reached for it again, and Guin relented. When Ynis looked up after a few moments, her mind had cleared somewhat. "It is nothing, right?"

"A scratch." Guin was lying.

As Ynis shifted the injured shoulder, she gasped in pain. "Son of—" She stopped herself this time. The muscle hadn't been cut deeply, she didn't think, but she wasn't going to be swinging her greatsword for a few days at least.

Guin squinted toward the creek, a worried look in their eye.

"Go make sure." Ynis grabbed Guin's wrist with her good hand and pulled herself up to standing. Her knee stung with another wound she hadn't noticed before. Blood seeped through the armor's knee joint, which had been pulled apart enough to let a claw through. In a standing fight, the geller had no chance against her, but if they fought dirty, they could be a real threat. Guin stared at Ynis' knee, then her shoulder, then her eyes, holding her gaze for a long moment. They blinked, then turned and stalked away, crossbow back in hand.

Ynis watched Guin move to the edge of the woods and stare out into the little valley for a long time. They moved along the edge of the forest, slow-stepping for stealth, which they actually had a chance at, being more lightly armored than Ynis. They stood watching for quite a while, then swapped out their crossbow for their broadsword and stalked out of sight into the valley. Ynis' breath grew shallow as she waited for what seemed an excessive amount of time. Whatever sound Guin's sword made sticking into the geller was swallowed by the babble of the creek. There were no snarls and no shouts, which had to be a good sign.

Ynis' eyes fluttered for a moment as scenes of the brief battle flashed through her mind: the frightened little deer galloping by; the *twang* of Guin's crossbow; the rush of green and grey streaking down from the trees. That was a new one. Geller weren't generally known for stealth when hunting in packs. Nor were they known to circle around and attack from the rear. Their position, with two in the valley and two in the woods, suggested strategy. Perhaps a pack of wolves with a good leader could mount a complex attack like that, but...

As Guin's head crested the lip of the valley, Ynis' attention swiveled back into the trees on instinct. The woods were dark with the coming dusk; ferns, stumps, and fallen trees made strange shapes in the shadows. Her eyes scanned each one, sure that a mind hid behind one of those silhouettes. Nothing moved. The only sound was the scrabble of Guin's boots on the valley edge and the low rush of the creek.

Guin approached slowly, having doubtless noticed what Ynis was doing. She felt their mass stand next to her, the warmth of their breath. Neither of them moved or spoke as the forest dimmed and finally darkened. Only the faint light from the fading sky above the creek allowed them to see the ground in front of them.

"We should climb back up to our horses before the light is gone entirely," Guin whispered. Ynis nodded, suddenly aware of the wound to her knee. It had mostly stopped bleeding, leaving her padding and left boot soaked and sticky with blood. All because she'd been bested by two measly geller.

Anger and self-loathing fueled her climb, helping her push past the astonishing pain in her shoulder. The weight of her armor alone put a constant strain on the wound, and the path required them to climb using branches or the trunks of saplings as handholds on several occasions. She managed not to curse or cry out, but it was a near thing.

It was fully night by the time they reached the bridge. A faint light pierced the thinning clouds, providing a ghostly view of the valley and the rushing creek. A wave of relief rushed through Ynis' chest at the sound of their horses nickering.

"Easy, girl." Sweetpea nosed in for a snort-kiss as she fondled the horse's ear. "That's right, momma's back." Sweetpea snuffled her shoulder, raising her head accusing-ly. "I'm fine, sweet girl. Don't you worry for a second." Sweetpea took quite a bit more convincing. Ynis lavished her with more praise and affection, until at last Sweetpea snorted in the way that meant "I'm ready to ride."

Guin was already in the saddle as Ynis struggled onto her horse using her one good arm. She bit down a scream at a stab of pain in her shoulder, settling for a hard sigh. "Just a scratch," she said, mostly to herself.

Guin's expression was hard to read in the dim light, but Ynis was sure it was a dubious one. "We should find a spot to camp and return to the castle in the morning, if you think you can ride."

"Return? Absolutely not. We've been sent on a mission, and I intend to see it through. I can fight with my left hand. I brought my broadsword as well." She reached across her body to pat the hilt.

It was a few moments before Guin responded. "As you command. We should ride a good way before we stop for the night. In case there are more. Are you..."

Ynis gripped the reins and turned the horse back in the direction they'd come from. "The forest past this plateau should offer shelter." She squeezed her legs against the horse's sides, and it took off at a gentle trot. She took the opportunity to grimace out of Guin's sight before they caught up.

Though they exchanged nary a word, Ynis felt Guin's worried glances as they rode into the gloomy night.

FOUR

Ynis snored lightly, a kind of fluttering purr. Guin had changed Ynis' dressing and re-applied antiseptic to her shoulder and knee before taking off her boots and tucking her in. Ynis had hardly argued, a sign of how tired she was and how *not* a scratch the wound was. Her boots, socks, and padding were sticky and crusted with dried blood, but neither wound was actively bleeding, which was something. Guin wiped out her boots as best they could and hung her crusty socks on a branch. Not that they'd dry much with the dew coming in overnight, but they might be fresher. They wished they could light a fire, but with geller about, it was out of the question.

The forest was dead silent, save the occasional hoot of an owl. If anything the size of a geller approached, they'd hear it, no matter how stealthy. They'd set up camp, such as it was, just inside the forest so the reflected starlight from the road allowed a dim view of the trees around. Guin leaned against a trunk and stared into the darkness of the woods, straining to make out one shadow from another. They forced themself to relax; looking harder wasn't going to do any good, and the forest's stillness was their best asset right now. They needed to keep themself in a state of calm readiness, just as they did in their nightly vigils, though it was geller they'd be watching out for, not the Angel. In time, they reached a state of peace with the darkness and the silence. If anything disturbed this space, they would know. Until then, all that remained was to keep their mind open and their body still.

It was impossible to tell the time without a view of the sky. After a while, they accepted this limitation; the mind could summon any manner of distraction if left free to roam. Time was irrelevant, so long as they stayed awake and aware of any change in their environment. They allowed their body to relax a little more. It had been a long day, and it would be a long night. Staying tense wouldn't help. *A loose mind is a supple mind*, their Teacher would always say, quoting one of the Angelite axioms. *An overwound trap springs itself*, said another. *To expect anything is to miss everything*. There were so many. They wove a gentle cocoon around Guin, helping them sink into the endless night.

The darkness seemed to shimmer for a moment, then billow like smoke. Guin watched, fascinated, as the shadows coalesced into a ragged form like a downward-pointing triangle descending from the trees. A cool breeze refreshed Guin's face, pulling a smile from their stupor. As the figure approached, it took shape: a winged being, a few shades lighter than the darkness, with a face like a cemetery statue gazing back from the Beyond.

She leaned down and reached out an ethereal grey hand, grazing their stubbled cheek with silky fingers. Shivers ran in icy webs along their jaw, across their scalp, and down their spine. What breath they might have had was trapped, unable to escape or be replenished as a dim light spread out from the Grey Angel, surrounding and suffusing them. For that was what it was, could only be. Guin gasped as She lifted their chin and their eyes met.

Silence. Light. Peace.

And then a terrible emptiness as She blinked, breaking the spell. Guin sobbed as Her fingers drew back, leaving a chill in their wake. They shivered head to toe as the Angel's energy ricocheted across their nerves. It was too much. It was everything. They needed so much more.

They gazed up at the Angel with tear-blurred eyes, releasing an ugly sob as She rose again into the branches. Her eyes stayed with Guin's as She ascended. Kind, understanding eyes. Eyes that saw through Guin's façade, through their very flesh, down to the seed they'd buried so long ago. Tendrils burst through the calcified shell and found fertile ground in their eager core. When at last the Grey Angel's dim light vanished into the treetops, Guin let out a stuttering sigh, releasing the next wave of tears.

They felt hollow, like a pitted olive. They touched their stubbled chin. This had only been a vision, hadn't it? Surely the Grey Angel hadn't visited Guin in the flesh. Whatever the case, after seeing Her...the world was different now. *Guin* was different. Their heart was as light as the wind and as heavy as the earth. Echoes of Her kindness, Her beauty, filtered through Guin like water seeping into cracked soil.

Deep below the surface, something began probing the void. It wasn't an unpleasant sensation, but rather like watching a spider plant's roots fill a jar. They settled in against the tree trunk, comforted by Ynis' soft snoring, and stared out into the shapeless dark as things they could only vaguely sense shifted inside them.

"Gods, I need to pee." Ynis winced as she pushed herself up to a sitting position. Lines from the pack she'd used as a pillow crisscrossed her face like ancient battle scars that only enhanced her stern beauty. Guin looked down as Ynis flashed them a grim smile, embarrassed to have been caught looking. "Do I look that bad?"

Guin let out a nervous chuckle. "No, just..." They made crisscross motions on their cheek, at which Ynis cocked her head in confusion. "You have marks from your pack." Guin gestured toward her face.

Ynis ran her fingers lightly over her cheek, which Guin imagined would be smooth to the touch, unlike their own now heavily stubbled cheeks. Ynis' fingers found the lines, tracing across them with a wry smile. "And you look like you've seen a ghost."

Guin looked down again. How could they tell Ynis about this? She didn't follow the Way. She wouldn't understand. Besides, had anything really happened, other than Guin having a vision? "Just tired, is all."

Ynis shot them a disbelieving look but said nothing as she shifted toward standing, grimacing and holding her knee. "Little help?"

Guin took her hand and hauled her to her feet. She was as heavy as she was strong, and with her knee in obvious pain, Guin had to put their back into it. Ynis put one hand against a tree, still wincing. "I should change your dressings and disinfect your wounds again. There's no telling what's on a geller's teeth."

"Don't forget the claws." She probed her knee, grimacing again, and took a hobbling step, then another. "Well, I'll be right back, assuming I can manage it in my condition."

"If you—" Guin shut their mouth, flushed with embarrassment, before Ynis waved them off.

"There's life in this girl yet." Her stride quickened, and Guin turned away, busying themself seeing to Wings of Night so as not to hear their mena's bodily functions.

"That's my girl," they murmured as the horse snorted warm breath in their ear. "That's my sweet dark angel."

"Sexy," Ynis said, ambling by in the way soldiers have when they're more hurt than they let on.

"I—what?" Guin's face and ears burned as they looked up at Ynis' smirking face.

"I'm just saying, if a woman spoke to me like that—" She shook her head, color rising in her cheeks, making her, impossibly, more attractive, and the situation infinitely more flustering. Had Ynis just called them a—"Sorry, I didn't mean—"

"You're fine," Guin managed, unsure if Ynis meant the sexual innuendo or the fact that she'd called Guin a woman. "I—I don't mind so much." In truth, they rather liked it, especially coming from Ynis, but it always felt like stolen valor.

Ynis' smile returned like the morning sun peeking over a mountain. "I'll keep that information tucked away for future reference."

"Not all the time, of course." Guin's ears were about to burst into flames.

"No, I totally get it." Ynis turned away, fishing a few carrots out of her saddlebag and tossing one to Guin. "But if you ever—"

"I will." Guin shook their head, but it brought no clarity. "I mean, not that I—" Guin stopped themself before they could dig the hole deeper.

Ynis groaned as she hoisted her pack up to attach it behind the saddle. She strapped it on tightly, then turned and leaned on her good knee with her good arm, breath heaving, giving Guin a good look at the crusty brown bandage. Finally, a distraction from this accursed conversation. Guin fished out the antiseptic and the last dressing from the medic kit. As she stood all the way back up, Ynis paused, staring at the bottle with tired eyes.

"Are we sure that's absolutely necessary?"

Guin scowled, eyeing her shoulder. "If you insist on continuing this mission without returning for proper medical treatment, you will at least let me tend to your wounds in the best way I can." Guin's voice rose in a way it seldom did, least of all with their mena.

One of Ynis' eyebrows arched imperiously. "Oh, I will, will I? I think I liked it better when you called me Mena and did what I said."

Guin hesitated, bottle and bandage held awkwardly between them. Gods, it almost felt like Ynis was *flirting* with them. Which was impossible, since—

Ynis' face fell, and she gave a nod. "Make it quick. We've got ten miles to ride before noon." She glanced around, then walked slowly to sit on a nearby fallen tree. Guin withheld a hiss as they removed the bandage and saw the yellow-tinged portion of the wound that heralded the beginning of an infection. "Well?" Ynis' voice was half irritated, half pleading.

"There's a spot of infection about the size of a pinky nail clipping. I'm going to bathe it as thoroughly as I can, so..."

Ynis tensed, then relaxed. Guin poured a careful splash onto the wound, which sizzled and bubbled around the infection. They put a gentle hand on Ynis' shoulder as she bucked against the pain.

"Cunt-shredding mother of unholy fuck!" Ynis growled through gritted teeth. She breathed hard through her nose then, after a few moments, through her mouth. A tear streaked down her miraculously clean cheek. Ynis was the only person Guin knew who could look like she just stepped out of the washroom while camping rough. Guin would have given anything to look half as put together as this on their best day. "Again," Ynis said, gripping the bark on the fallen tree. Guin poured out another splash, and the wound bubbled a bit less this time.

"Fucking nasty-ass geller *fucks!* I will fucking *murder* you down to the last greasy whelp fresh-hatched from its bitch-mother's cunt," she hissed. "I will dig up your ancestors' bones and burn them on a bonfire!"

Guin bit their lip to hide their smirk as they carefully placed the bandage. Ynis only winced a little as they tucked it snugly under the torn padding on both sides. Guin gently laid her shoulder plate back on, only tightening the straps enough to keep it from falling off.

Ynis stood with a harsh sigh, then cracked a half-smile. "Sorry about all the swearing. Not very fitting for a mena."

"Plenty fitting for a soldier, if you ask me."

Ynis shook her head, sucking her teeth. "I'm supposed to provide an example. I can't go whining every time I get a scratch."

"It's a bite, not a scratch, and a pretty nasty one at that. I wonder if it's too late to put a few stitches in it."

"No time." Ynis groaned as she hoisted herself back onto her horse, jaw clenched against what must have been some serious pain. "You can sew it up tonight if you like."

"I don't like sewing up wounds that would best be tended to by a proper medic," Guin groused as they mounted Wings of Night. "And I'm not very good with a needle. But I will do as I am asked."

Ynis' quirked smile set Guin's heart on edge. She guided her horse onto the road and gave a soldier's nod. "Let's ride."

They reached the game trails before noon. The ground was dry and firm and the undergrowth sparse, and the horses made their way through easily enough. Ynis stopped to examine tracks a few times, though she did not dismount; no doubt the pain kept her in her saddle. Guin noticed tracks of boar, several kinds of deer, and a few smaller mammals, but nothing like the distinctive clawed two-and-two marks of the geller's loping stride. Their claws didn't seem to be retractable, which would make them more like a wolf than a wood lion, Guin mused. At any rate, there were none to be seen in the muddy spots around the springs, so they kept moving.

As they crested a small ridge, Ynis stopped abruptly, holding a half-closed fist at her side. She'd sensed something. Wings of Night must have seen the signal before Guin did; she stopped and stood still, without so much as a snort. They couldn't see over the ridge, as they'd been riding behind Ynis when she stopped. Ynis' head turned slowly, as if she were scanning the forest. Guin could picture the stern, slitted look on her face. Either she had exceptional eyesight, or she was just better at noticing things, or both; she always saw what others missed.

After what looked like a full scan from one side to the other and back, she tugged on the reins and turned her horse around. Wings followed suit before Guin could signal the turn, and they made their way quietly back to the bottom of the next valley before Ynis hissed the stop signal. Guin turned halfway around. Ynis rode up alongside them, Sweetpea trampling ferns and pinecones in the underbrush. Guin smiled every time they pictured Ynis naming her horse that. She met Ynis' eyes, which looked fully alive again for the first time since her injury.

"On the opposite ridge, I think, maybe halfway up. Just the one." She sucked her teeth and gave a little shake of her head. "I didn't see it, but I *felt* it. It saw me for sure. Not you, maybe."

"Geller?" Guin whispered, suddenly seized with fear, though they'd slain dozens of the creatures.

Ynis nodded once, her face a mask of stone. "There's something different about this one."

Guin swallowed and nodded. The lone geller were thought to be wilier than those that ran in packs. The dark fire in Ynis' eyes told Guin she'd embraced this challenge, been invigorated by it. Guin felt only a deepening pit in their stomach.

"What's our play?" they asked.

"My leaving signaled to it that I respect its territory." She glanced over her shoulder at the ridge. "Where we go, it will follow. It will attack us if it thinks us vulnerable and steer clear if it thinks us strong."

Guin glanced at Ynis' shoulder, then at her knee, then back up into her eyes, which were hard like blackwood. There was no way she would leave without killing the creature, or it killing her. "Which would you prefer?"

"Well, I look the part of the victim, don't I? Barring the armor, of course. But that's less relevant for the kind of attack I expect it to use."

"So, you want to be bait?"

"It's either that or try to hunt it down in its own backyard while nursing an infected wound." She lifted her shoulder gently, grimacing at the pain. "We ride on a little way, but not too far." She gestured back toward where they'd come from. "Set up camp, clean this damned wound again. It will observe us tonight; my instinct says it won't attack until tomorrow, but you never know."

Guin dropped their eyes, chewing on their lip. This was a terrible plan, especially in Ynis' condition. She was already risking serious infection by not being back at the castle. Another two days might be life-threatening.

"Soldier," Ynis barked quietly. "Speak your piece."

Guin breathed in deeply through their nose. They had no choice but to answer honestly. "I think it's a poor plan, Mena." If Ynis was going to call them soldier, Guin had free rein to use her title. "If we don't stop the infection—which, with only half a bottle of antiseptic left, we probably won't—it could spread internally."

Ynis sniffed noisily. "I have a famously strong constitution."

"And a famously stubborn heart when you set your mind to your prey." The corner of Guin's mouth lifted despite their efforts to stop it. Ynis wasn't going back. The shine in her eyes told them the battle was lost.

In truth, it had been lost when Guin first set eyes on Ynis in her debut public tournament. She'd ridden out into the arena, hair rippling behind her like living shadow, strong arm holding her sword up to gleam in the sun. She'd scanned the crowd with her eyes, as if daring anyone to doubt that she would be victorious. She'd lost the match on points, but that hadn't stopped Guin from losing their heart. Everything they'd done since then was for a chance to ride at her side, to bask in her confidence, her beauty.

It wasn't so much that they were attracted to her; everyone was. Being in her presence made Guin feel...more like themself somehow. But a better self, a self more like Ynis than like—

"You're pensive."

"I am not," Guin replied instinctively, as one who's nodded off denies having been asleep. "I'm just...thinking."

Ynis' eyebrow arched and her lips formed a dubious moue. Gods, when had she found the time to apply lipstick? The earthy mauve looked almost natural, giving just a hint of intrigue to her already fascinating lips. "Think while you ride, soldier." Ynis winked, adding fluster to Guin's consternation. Ynis set out at a quick trot, so Guin had no time to sit with their thoughts.

That was probably for the best. The more they thought about Ynis, the less worthy they felt to be in her presence.

FIVE

Ynis winced as Guin probed around her wound with gentle fingers. "It's too late for stitches," Guin said, then explored further in silence.

"What about the infection?" Guin's long hesitation before answering told her everything their words didn't.

"I think the antiseptic is helping." They removed their fingers and rustled around in the medic kit. The now-familiar sound of the lid being unscrewed had Ynis gripping the mossy stump she was sitting on. "Ready?"

Ynis nodded, lying. "Aaah bitch-fucker from the devil's taint!" she growled, trying not to scream as she shook from the searing pain in her shoulder. "Fuck your crusty ass with a morningstar!"

Guin's snort broke the tension. Ynis breathed out, long and slow, as the pain ebbed to a raging throb. "And again,"

Guin said in a low, soft voice. The pain was blinding this time, robbing Ynis of the ability to spew the profanity that normally helped her cope. Sudden tears burst forth, along with an ugly sob.

"Shh-shh-shh-shh." Guin put a gentle hand on her back. Ynis sobbed a few more times until her breath settled in a stuttering sigh. She leaned away from Guin's hand. They stepped back with an expression like pity masked as concern.

"I'm fine, I just...*fuck*." Ynis felt around for her handkerchief, but it was nowhere to be found. She accepted Guin's, which was neatly folded and as clean as the moment it had come out of the laundry. It even retained a whiff of the lavender soap. "Thank you," she said, after ruining it on her eyes and nose. She folded it back into a square and tucked it into a pocket. "I'll give you mine when I find it."

"I have another." Guin was staring at her knee now. They approached, crouching next to her to examine the wound. Their fingers pulled away the torn padding and mail and they closed in further trying to get a look at it. They sat back on their heels, shaking their head. "I don't *think* it's infected, but the tear in the armor's pretty small, so it's hard to get a good look."

Ynis bit back a smirk, and the quip that leapt to her tongue about how if Guin wanted to get into her pants, they should try buying her dinner first. It was the kind of joke soldiers made, but not Guin. Never Guin. They were too...respectable for that sort of thing, too solid. A being made of wood or stone, unaffected by life's frivolity.

"Well, I need to get out of this stinking padding and give it a good wash in that stream." Ynis had picked this spot to return to for that reason. "Help me with my back and shoulder plates?"

Guin stood behind her, unbuckling and removing pieces of armor in silence. They moved around to the front and lifted the breastplate gently off. Her wound felt much better without that weight. If she could manage to get out of her hauberk without passing out, it would be like being freed from a cage. She started to do it herself, but the pain was too great. Guin stepped in without a word, lifting Ynis' sleeves one at a time and helping her slither out of them. Tears came to her eyes again as she moved her bad shoulder, but the sudden release when the weight of the mail was off was worth every agonizing moment.

She stood gasping as Guin removed her padding, leaving her in a stinking, blood-stained tunic. Guin knelt without further ado and removed the armor and mail from her legs, then helped her out of her padding. The dusk air was cool but invigorating through her thin underlayers. She took a deep breath, then let it out. Her knee was starting to throb as well, but she had no time for scratches. "Thank you."

Guin eyed the surroundings nervously, hand on the pommel of their sword.

"Might want to keep the crossbow handy," Ynis said as she gathered her padding, a bar of soap, her dagger, and her meager face towel, which was going to be doing some heavy lifting. Guin stood, crossbow now in hand, eyes scanning the forest, only briefly flashing toward Ynis, as if she were already naked. She'd always suspected Guin had a thing for her—most women did. Most *people*, she reminded herself. It felt rude to think of Guin as a woman when they'd never claimed to be one, but it was hard not to.

It wasn't her business. Nor was Guin's potential crush. Ynis glanced back at them several times while washing; Guin remained fixed on their surroundings, as if actively avoiding looking at her. She washed her padding as well as possible in the stream's icy waters. If it rained, she was fucked because she couldn't wear armor over wet padding or over no padding at all. They'd have to risk a fire. It wasn't like the geller didn't know where they were.

She glanced back again before shedding her underclothes. Guin's eyes scanned the forest like a hunting dog's, but they did seem to flicker toward Ynis as she pulled her undershirt over her head and stepped out of her pants. She felt oddly uncomfortable as she crouched, naked and covered in gooseflesh, to scrub the worst of the blood out of her clothes. This was nothing unusual; she bathed with other soldiers all the time. Why did this feel different? She freshened up with a few careful wipes across her face, neck, and pits, keeping the water well clear of her wounds. Streams like this carried all sorts of nasties in them from animal feces upstream.

She sighed as she realized she'd have to put her streamwater-soaked shirt on right over the wound. She tore the gash wider in several directions, cursing as the movement triggered a fresh spike of pain in her shoulder. She cursed a bit more as she wrestled into the cold, wet clothes, which stuck to her like a coat of freezing rain. Her teeth began to chatter as she put on her boots and picked up the rest of her belongings. She felt a little better once the dagger was in her hand; better still when she stood next to Guin, grim and fierce in the dwindling light.

"Get a fire going," she said through chattering teeth. She reached for the crossbow, which Guin relinquished with a gentle blink. Ynis cleared a patch of ground for the fire with her boots, generating a little heat as Guin scoured the forest for fuel. Within minutes, the crackle of burning pine branches broke the forest's quiet. Ynis moved in as close as she dared, spreading her arms around the fire to soak up every bit of heat. Guin soon returned with more substantial pieces of wood. After a bit of chopping and splitting, they had the fire blazing so hot Ynis had to step back and turn around.

"Gods, does that feel good." The front of her under-clothes had nearly dried already, and she felt the steam rising up her neck from the back. She tried to focus on the forest, but there wasn't much to see beyond the circle of light from their fire.

Guin rounded the fire to stand next to her. "Not to state the obvious, but aren't you worried about the geller finding us?"

"I'm counting on it. It would have found us regardless. It no doubt followed us at a distance after we left."

Guin stood silent for a long moment, then picked up Ynis' padding and propped it up with sticks near the fire. "You should sleep. I'll stand watch."

"All night? You'll be useless in the morning. We do shifts, just like normal."

Guin moved the padding a little farther from the fire; it had started to steam. "I'll take first shift."

"I was hoping you'd say that." Ynis turned back around to roast her front side, blinking thanks at Guin as she did. "But don't be a hero. Wake me at half morn."

Guin nodded. The odds they would obey that command were less than fifty-fifty, and the odds that Ynis would object if they disobeyed were far lower.

They ate a grim meal of jerky and hardcakes, which never sat well with Ynis. In fairness, the greasy fruit-and-nut cakes didn't sit well with anyone, but they kept for weeks and gave enough energy to get a soldier through the day without collapsing. Guin gathered more wood as Ynis unrolled her sleep pocket and fluffed the pillow end, crossbow ever pointed toward the dark woods.

She swished a bit of water around her mouth and swallowed it, then lay her broadsword, dagger, and crossbow on the ground next to her sleep pocket. "Wake me for anything," she said as she slipped in between the layers. "Anything," she repeated, locking eyes with Guin.

Guin nodded, crossbow in hand, lit up like a statue of fire and shadow, hard eyes staring off into the darkness.

Guin snored, a soft, sputtering noise, not an unpleasant sound. At one point she—*they*! Godsdammit, Ynis needed to stop. It was just that there was something in the way they looked at her, an envy different from the usual. They desired her; of that there could be no doubt. The way they averted their eyes, the stony respect in their tone, the soft quarter-smile that bloomed when she looked at them. But it was more than that. A look Ynis had seen a dozen times, the pining of a soul trapped in the body of another.

She sighed. Not her business.

The forest was empty, silent as a root cellar. Nothing moved in the featureless dark beyond the firelight. And yet, as Ynis gazed into the void, she knew golden-grey eyes were watching her, obscured by foliage and ferns.

Guin's sleepy shifting by the fire drew her attention. As she watched, Guin's body stiffened, and they began trembling. Ynis stepped closer and saw their eyes wide and wild, their mouth stretched in awe. Was this one of those religious things the Angelites believed in? They chased visions of some mystical Grey Angel said to grant wisdom or even wishes. The most revered among them claimed to have been visited. Some disappeared for weeks, only to return, dazed and fatigued but otherwise sound, unable to remember (or perhaps unwilling to divulge) what had happened during their time away. Guin's eyes were open, pupils twitching up and down; they certainly weren't aware of Ynis' presence. After a time, they rasped a loud sigh, releasing the tremble of their body, and their eyes fluttered closed.

Ynis' head whipped around of its own accord and her crossbow followed. Ten yards into the forest, two yellow orbs glinted in the firelight, then disappeared. Ynis scanned with her eyes and bow, but there was nothing to be seen. A glance back at Guin confirmed they were settling back to sleep after whatever strange dream state they'd been in.

Nothing moved in the dark woods; the only sound was the low crackling hum of the fire. Ynis settled into a relaxed readiness, tossing another quarter-log on the coals as she scanned the darkness all around. As long as she didn't get caught with her guard down, she'd have a shot with the crossbow and time to pull her broadsword, though she would be slower with her left hand. She practiced the movement a few times, wincing as pain flared in her shoulder. It was warmer than it should be, which was never a good sign. But there was no time to cry about it with a geller stalking them in the dark. She was the mena, after all.

Morning arrived in a haze of fatigue, accompanied by the aches heralding sickness. Guin's grim eyes as they changed the bandage spoke volumes. "You must go back."

Ynis shook her head. "One more day and night. If we have not brought down the creature by then, I will agree to return."

Guin stood stiffly, taking on their military face. "Mena, if this doesn't get treated by a proper medic, you will most definitely die."

"Surely not in a day!"

"Ynis," Guin said in a soft voice that twisted something in her chest. "Please."

"Guin." She put a hand on their shoulder. "Put some antiseptic on it. We ride after breakfast."

Ynis rode slowly, studying the ground as she went. She'd found geller tracks in a muddy patch near their camp, but something didn't feel right. The creature had shown itself to her on purpose, as a taunt. It was smart enough to play mind games, and surely smart enough not to step in mud where it would leave marks. They followed the nearest game trail, looking for any sign of the creature's passage. It was to no avail, but Ynis *knew* they were on the right track.

Guin had been laconic all morning, even for them. Ynis had asked if they'd slept well, hoping to tease something out, but Guin had just grumbled, "As well as can be expected."

Ynis left them to their brooding, or meditation, or whatever it was. It was annoying. She needed someone to lift her spirits, not shroud them both in a fog of discontent. They crossed a lowland bog at the foot of a valley, hoping to pick up the trail. Ynis grew hot when the sun hit her, then cold when she paused under the shade of a scrub cedar to mop her forehead.

"You should eat." Guin pulled a piece of jerky out of their pouch and offered it. Ynis waved it away; the mere sight of it made her want to lose what little was left in her stomach. Guin shrugged and tore at it with their teeth.

Ynis sighed. "You're right. But I don't fancy either jerky or hardcakes right now. My stomach's a little sour." In truth, it was a lot sour, but Guin didn't need to know that.

Guin fished around in their saddlebag and pulled out a wooden box. "What about a sweetbiscuit?" They opened the box toward her, revealing six perfect sweetbiscuits, their crinkled edges intact thanks to a checkered napkin lining the box. "I forgot about them in all the chaos."

"Gods, you're a lifesaver." The biscuit was crunchy on the outside, with those big grains of sugar, and soft on the inside, almost creamy. "Mmm. I can't believe they're still fresh."

"It's the napkin. Kollian wool. Keeps the humidity regular."

"I bet they made you unit leader in Fledglings."

Guin quirked a smile, still holding out the box. "They made me wait until I was twelve. Said I was too quiet to be a leader." They shook their head wistfully.

"Is that why you're still a squaddie?" Ynis eyed the box, then blinked it away. The mush in her mouth that had been a delicious sweetbiscuit moments ago was suddenly making her queasy.

Guin's eyes furrowed as they carefully folded the napkin back over the biscuits and put the box away. "I'm just happy to do my part. I don't need anyone depending on me."

"And yet here I am, needing your help to do every damned thing." Ynis swallowed with a wince, eyeing the half biscuit in her hand. She needed the energy. She took a careful swig of water, then forced another bite down.

"First Principles, Men—Ynis. Sorry." They ducked their head a little.

"First Principles." *Do for others when you can; accept from others when you must.* Ynis hated the idea that an entire society had to live by the same philosophy, even a good one. She steeled herself for the final bite, washing it down with a generous glug of water. "What if the Queendom needed your experience, your calm in the face of danger? Would you be willing to command a squad? To *do for others*, as it were?" Ynis hadn't given it much thought before, but Guin would make an excellent commander if they just had a little confidence in themself.

"I'm happy where I am." Guin squinted at Ynis, then dropped their eyes again, their tan cheeks flushing toward red. "But I'll go where I'm told."

"Well, I won't push it, but you should think about it. Meanwhile, I'm happy where you are as well. I can't think of anyone I'd trust with my life more than you."

"Same." Guin turned back toward the saddlebag, rummaged around, and brought out an apple. They studiously cut a slice off with their knife and offered it to Ynis without looking directly into her eyes. She took it, though she didn't want it. It was pleasant enough, scraping the remains of the biscuit away and leaving her mouth feeling a tad less pasty. They finished the apple in silence, Guin cutting off a slice at a time. Ynis ate one more slice, then waved away the rest. Guin made short work of the remaining slices, then wiped their knife and sheathed it, eyeing the bog ahead. It was filled with clumps of tall grass, small thickets, and other places a geller could hide. Ynis doubted it would attack two mounted soldiers in broad daylight, but she couldn't afford to let her guard down.

They moved slowly along the bog trail, which grew muddy as they approached the little stream flowing down from the valley. The trail crossed the stream on an old spadetooth dam, which she didn't trust to support the weight of their horses. The mud beside the dam wouldn't hold either, but it wasn't deep enough to be a problem. As they crossed the stream and emerged onto the muddy bank on the other side, Ynis saw them: a set of two geller tracks, then another pair, as if it had scampered out of the water and made off along a smaller game trail running through the grass alongside the stream. She pointed them out silently, and Guin nodded, staring up the valley.

"This leads up past Highneck Ridge, if memory serves."

Ynis nodded. "All the way up to Wicked Peak, according to the map." The peak lurked in the background, probably two days' ride away, depending on how far up the horses could go. It was one of the taller foothills, pocked with caves said to have been made by burning boulders raining down from the sky. Ynis eyed Guin, who surely wouldn't be happy about her trekking farther away from the castle's medics.

"You said one more night, so we'd better get moving," they said instead, an unexpected edge of almost-eagerness in their voice.

Ynis nudged Sweetpea toward the path. Guin fell in behind, crossbow now slung over their chest. They didn't see any more tracks as they followed the trail up out of the marsh and into drier, rocky terrain studded with copses of cedar as well as thickets of winterbrush whose berries were just starting to turn red as the nights grew cool. They dismounted to give their legs a stretch and let the horses drink from the stream. Ynis wobbled a bit as she first set her feet down, but she forced herself steady to avoid Guin's concerned glances. Her head felt thick, as if she were fending off a hangover, and not particularly well. She became more aware of the constant throbbing in her shoulder, which sent pulses of searing heat down her arm.

"I wonder how it sees us." Guin's voice startled Ynis, who was lost in self-pity.

"The geller?"

Guin nodded, making as if to spit, then swallowed. An oddly delicate gesture for a soldier. "Does it know what we are? Or does it just see us as dangerous animals?"

"Hard to blame it for that, I suppose." Ynis hadn't really given it much thought; the geller were beasts to be slain to protect the citizens of the Queendom. If this one really was smarter than the others, able to observe them and decide if and when to attack, did that make it...something closer to human?

"I don't want to be dangerous," Guin said glumly. "I hate the sight of their corpses. Their faces..."

"Yeah." The creatures did have more in common with humans than any other animal Ynis had ever seen. "In answer to your question...I guess the one we're tracking knows or has figured out what we are and what we intend to do to it. And if I were in its shoes, well, its paws, I'd take any chance I could to kill us before we kill it."

Guin nodded, squinting up the valley. "I figure we have a good quarter-day before we'd have to set up camp, if you're..."

Ynis stood from the rock she was sitting on, slowly to minimize the rush of blood to her head. She clicked her cheek, and Sweetpea raised her head from the stream, ears flicking in attention. "Let's see if we can't find more tracks a little farther up. And if we find nothing by nightfall, and nothing...happens during the night, we ride back."

SIX

Guin found a nice copse of cedar with a bit of a clear spot in the middle for their camp. They'd seen what looked like another set of geller tracks toward evening, though with the rocky ground, it was harder to be sure.

Ynis had promised to return the next morning, but after their visit from the Grey Angel the night before, Guin was feeling unsettled about the idea of giving up. She hadn't communicated with words, but the look in Her eyes had seemed to be beckoning Guin forward. Her call was hard to resist. Ynis' infection was spreading slowly, but she barely had a fever and didn't seem to be significantly worse than the previous evening. The bottle of antiseptic was only a quarter full now, maybe enough to stave off the worst of the infection for a couple more days.

As they watched over Ynis sleeping by the fire, Guin marveled at the curve of her hips, visible even beneath her sleep pocket, so different from Guin's flat, angular body. They steeled their mind, trying to keep it from returning to the moment they'd seen Ynis naked, bending to wash her shirt in the stream, breasts squished against her knees, the slit of her womanhood running neatly along a trim line of hair between her rounded buttocks. Guin knew Ynis had been Shaped, but the sight of her body, no different than any other woman's, sparked a desire they'd long kept tamped down.

Most of the time, Guin didn't mind the parts they had; they even came in handy when sleeping with women who liked to be penetrated. Other times, they struggled to maintain their desire long enough for the act, at least that part of it. Worshiping a woman with their hands and mouth was one thing—a marvelous, miraculous thing—but using their cock sometimes felt like a betrayal. It shouldn't be that way; their parts didn't define who Guin was. And yet...

They shook off this unproductive line of thought and focused their eyes on the terrain around them, dimly lit by cloud-muffled stars. The silence was different here; the distant gurgle of the stream replaced the gentle rustle of leaves from the previous night in the forest. They imagined the geller stalking them, watching for their attention to flag. Guin gripped their crossbow tighter, back to the fire, gazing out into the grey shadows of the mountainside. A slice of moon rose from behind Wicked Peak, adding a ghostly sheen to the rocks and limning the trees with silver. The cedar fronds, in this light, reminded them of the Angel's wings, luminous grey against the dark sky.

Guin shivered. The previous night's visitation tugged at their heart like tiny wires, pulling up, ever up. Did the peak have the shape of a wing? Surely it was a flight of fancy, but they couldn't shake it. Neither could they shake the look in Her eyes, a kind, almost pitying encouragement. *Come to me*, She seemed to say; *Come and be made whole.*

It wasn't a sound so much as a feeling that spun Guin around to see a dark shape slink out of the nearest copse. It froze as they trained their crossbow on it, until all they could see were the golden slits of its eyes. The eyes vanished, and a shadow materialized in the air. Guin's crossbow went off with a *twang*. A snarl erupted as the geller tumbled to the ground at their feet.

It was up in an instant, lunging for them in a flurry of claws and teeth. Guin whacked it in the head with the butt of their crossbow, then spun out of the way and pushed off as the claws fought for purchase on their mail sleeves. It landed in the edge of the fire and leapt away with a squeal of pain. Ynis was on her feet, swaying with broadsword in hand.

The creature bounded toward her, and Guin leapt over the fire, drawing their broadsword just enough to hit it in the chest with the pommel. They tumbled to the ground, wrapped around each other. The geller's claws pulled Guin in as its teeth gnashed around the blade they managed to get between them. A thud sounded, and the beast rolled away with a squeal, then vanished in a scrabble of rock and dust. Ynis stood over Guin, gazing down with worried eyes.

"I'm fine." Guin ignored Ynis' outstretched hand and pushed up to standing, eyeing the direction the geller had fled. It had disappeared behind a copse and could be a hundred yards away by now, or it could be lurking and catching its breath. "Damn, but those things are quick."

"Are you hurt?"

Guin shook their head, inspecting the spots where their ribs and neck stung a bit. The claws hadn't pierced the mail, but they'd have bruises. "I got caught by surprise. I won't miss next time."

"You hit it." Ynis pointed her sword toward a splash of blood on the ground that led to a trail of drops in the creature's wake. "I saw the bolt in its shoulder when I kicked it. Didn't want to risk swinging this with you two rolling around like that." She half-lifted her sword apologetically.

"Hopefully that will keep it off our asses for the rest of the night." Guin retrieved their crossbow, which was dusty but otherwise intact. They wiped it clean and reloaded.

"Well, I'm awake now, so you might as well get some sleep. Just as soon as I visit the facilities." She went behind a nearby bush, and it was all Guin could do not to follow her to make sure the geller wasn't around. Ynis was no fool; she'd scout the area before leaving herself vulnerable. She was back moments later, carrying another branch for the fire. She braced it against the ground and broke it with a loud crack. Guin winced at the noise, not that it mattered at this point.

Guin took a sip of water, then laid out their weapons next to their sleep pocket and slid between the layers. They doubted they'd be able to sleep after all the excitement, but they had to try. Maybe their mind-clearing would help. Maybe the Angel would visit them again.

"You still awake?" Ynis said in a low voice after a while. Guin slitted their eyes open to see her leaning over them, broadsword in hand.

"Can't really sleep after all that."

"Yeah. You should, though."

Guin grunted in response. The fire crackled, and Ynis circled it in slow steps, stopping periodically. Guin couldn't see her with their eyes closed, but they could almost feel her presence as she passed by again. It was distracting at first, then reassuring. Guin used each circle around the fire as an anchor, clearing a little more space in their mind with each pass. They were as safe as they could be in the circumstances. After a time, behind closed lids they saw the stars above, shining bright beyond the veil of cloud. The moon, a bigger wedge than last night, biding her time until she was ready to give birth to the sun. As it always was and ever would be, long after humans had vanished from the land.

The moon's face grew darker; a shadow bloomed in the center, spreading out to block her light. The shadow grew wings and took on a form like an ancient statue of a goddess, soft curves hardened into permanence. Her face was at once familiar and foreign, a benevolent mother from another time, another world.

There was a sharpness in Her eye, a hunger; the touch of Her hand on Guin's cheek sparked something like desire deep within them. As the Grey Angel lifted their chin and their eyes met, Guin fell into Her, swirling like a leaf in a drain. A whooshing sound, a quickening as they rushed through a dark channel and into the void, like going over a waterfall and landing in the sky. Guin's mind split apart at the seams, drifting among the stars, becoming part of the infinite galaxy of uncountable joy. In that moment, she felt—

Guin gasped as they sat bolt upright, staring into the space where the Angel had been. Ynis was at their side in a moment, strong hand on their shoulder.

"Did you see it again?" she whispered.

Guin swiveled their head toward Ynis, who gazed down with knowing eyes. *Again*. How did she know? Had she seen it too? Guin nodded.

"Did it...did it say anything?

"She," Guin managed, still reeling from the sharp jerk back to reality. "And no, She never talks. She just..." Those eyes, the way She saw Guin, saw through them, like She was studying the dimensions of Guin's soul. "She just looks at me. And I feel...seen."

"Is She beautiful?"

A tear escaped Guin's eye. "Yes," they whispered, heart aching as the vision faded. Guin had to see Her again, to bask in Her gaze, to feel, just for a moment, that someone saw them as—

"I wish I could see Her." Ynis wasn't religious as far as Guin knew; certainly not an Angelite, but she used a reverent tone when speaking of Her now. "I wish I could see what you see."

"It takes time and patience...so much patience. But you could, if you truly wanted to." Guin hated proselytizing, but Ynis had shown curiosity. It was part of the Angelite code to speak of the practice to those who'd expressed interest.

Ynis stood and turned away, shaking her head. "Patience is not one of my virtues, insofar as I can be said to have any."

"You've been more than patient with me and the other squaddies."

Ynis heaved a single chuckle. "I've been tested for sure."

"And you never snap, never tear someone's head off because they screw up in the heat of the moment. That is a rare quality."

"You don't know how close—" Ynis smiled, shaking her head. "Thank you." Guin nodded acknowledgment, a gesture far too subtle for the swell of emotions inside them. "Now see if you can get back to sleep."

"Not likely." Guin snuggled down inside their sleep pocket. The air did have a bit of a nip to it, and it was rather cozy in there. Maybe the Angel would visit them in their dreams. And if not, maybe Ynis would.

Guin winced as they sprinkled antiseptic onto Ynis' wound. The infection was definitely spreading around the rim, which had turned red and angry. If she didn't get back soon—Guin shook their head, not giving the thought room to emerge. Ynis was tough. They sprinkled a little more on, being extra careful, since they were almost out. After tonight, maybe tomorrow morning, there would be none left, nothing to keep the wound from burrowing into her body and ravaging her from the inside out.

They followed the trail of blood while it lasted, which was not long. It must have been a flesh wound. Guin had been lucky to hit it at all in the dark with it flying through the air like that. They found a few tracks here and there, but it was slow work; the creature seemed to be zigzagging on purpose to throw them off.

One thing was for sure: It was headed uphill. At some point it seemed to have entered the stream, so they each took a side and rode slowly, studying the ground for any signs. Guin spotted a bit of a game trail leading through a thicket and followed it. It led to a cluster of scrub trees, then continued uphill, passing from one clump of vegetation to the next. They didn't see any tracks, but it was tricky with the dry ground, especially on horseback.

They waved Ynis over, watching how she rode as Sweet-pea picked her way across the stream. Her posture was stiff, a little off-center, as if she was trying to protect her shoulder from too much jostling. She raised her eyebrows hopefully, but Guin blinked no. They gestured toward the trail, which Ynis was already following with her eyes.

"Anything like this on the other side?" they asked.

Ynis shook her head, wincing as she dismounted awkwardly. "It's almost certain to use the trail, especially as it's injured."

"Unless it's holed up somewhere to the side, waiting for us to pass so it can come up behind us." Guin joined Ynis on the ground, patting Wings' neck and holding her reins gently.

Ynis shook her head. "It won't attack us at our strongest, even from behind. And you notice how it keeps going uphill?"

Guin grunted affirmation and chewed on their lip. It was strange for a wounded creature to expend more energy going uphill unless it was headed for certain shelter or more of its kind. "It's not just running from us. It's running to—" A tingle flared in Guin's mind, and they closed their eyes. The Angel flashed in their vision, soaring down the mountainside in the silver moonlight.

"What?" Ynis' voice was soft, curious.

"I don't—I..." Guin shook their head. It was just their mind playing tricks on them. It didn't mean, couldn't mean anything.

"I'd have you tell me whatever it is you saw, however strange or irrelevant it may seem." Ynis' voice rose, taking on the timbre of command.

Another tingle flared, in Guin's heart this time. "I saw Her, flying down the mountain at night. Just for a moment, then..." They strained to summon the image again. Her wings were dark with shadow beneath and shining silver on top. Her hair flowed behind Her in eloquent waves, and—was that a tail whipping behind Her? The vision was fading, and it was impossible to be sure, but there had been something...They took one last look as the image dimmed beyond recollection; the only thing still visible was a perfect slice of quarter moon. They snapped their fingers. "How many days till the quarter moon?"

"Tomorrow night," Ynis answered without hesitation.

"That's when I'll see Her," Guin realized as they said it. "That's what She's been trying to tell me. I have to keep going." They steeled their jaw as they took in Ynis' face, a little paler than usual, her rich bronze skin faded to yellow gold. She didn't show any signs of fever, and her energy level was good, but two days up, then all the way back, in her condition? It might well kill her.

"*We* have to keep going." Ynis stuck out a finger at Guin's chest. "Better we send the horses back and track it on foot." She unbuckled her pack and slung it over one shoulder, struggling to reach the dangling strap with her bad arm. Guin took the strap and came around front, standing perilously close to Ynis' curved breastplate. "Thanks," Ynis breathed as Guin secured it to the other strap as best they could. They would have offered to carry both packs, but they knew what Ynis' response would be.

Guin pulled on their own pack and slung their crossbow awkwardly at their side. "Mena, I have to ask. Your wound is worsening, and we'll run out of antiseptic soon. Is it really worth risking your life for one geller?"

"*Fuck* that geller." Her eyes were unusually animated; perhaps she was feverish after all. "When we find it, we kill it."

"And if it finds us?"

"We kill it."

"And if your infection worsens and you die out here on the mountain, away from all your kin?"

"You kill it, then bury me as befits a warrior who died in the service of the Queendom."

Guin covered their face with their hand. "I still don't see how—"

"Did you or did you not have visions of the elusive Grey Angel everyone's always going on about?"

"Yes, but I—"

"Let me ask you something: Do you believe what you saw? Do you believe that the literal Grey Angel, which you've been obsessing about your whole life, visited you in your dreams and in your waking mind?"

"Yes," Guin whispered, more certain of this than they'd ever been of anything in their life. They finally understood those who'd had the visions, who'd gone away and come back changed. Guin had been chosen, gods knew why, but they *had*.

"How is this even a question, then? You get one chance in your life for something like this. *One*. Hells, I never believed any of this stuff before, but now? Seeing you, the way you..." She waved her hand in the air around Guin, voice softening as she continued. "You're practically glowing." Guin turned their face down to hide the deep flush of color they knew had risen. "I want to see your face when you finally lay eyes on Her."

They sent their horses on their way home with a note for the Haemene and resumed their climb on foot. The valley narrowed as the grade steepened, the water tumbling white over endless rocks. By noon they were in a sort of canyon, following a narrow path along the stream's edge. They saw another set of geller tracks in a muddy patch, and a spot in the sand where it appeared to have sat. Perhaps it was tiring in its wounded state. Guin was so lost in thought that she almost ran into Ynis, who'd stopped and held up her hand as they neared a bend in the stream. Guin scanned the steep slopes on either side of them and the place where the path curved around the bend but saw nothing. They sidled up next to Ynis and cast a concerned glance at her. Ynis started to form a word with her lips, which were, incredibly, freshly painted in that earthy mauve, when her mouth dropped open, and her eyes darted up the cliff.

The crack and tumble of rock sounded above. Guin glanced up to see a chunk of the cliff collapse, even as their body moved of its own accord to tackle Ynis to the path. A great sharp weight drove into their back, chasing the breath from their lungs before their scream of pain could begin. Another struck their leg, a third their head, and a hail of smaller rocks thumped and clattered down all around. Guin lay dazed in the ringing silence that followed, unable to draw breath or move from where they were sprawled over Ynis.

"Guin," Ynis groaned as she pushed up from beneath them, finally rolling them onto their back. Guin's chest refused to lift, their lungs stuck together like sheets of wet paper. "Guin!" Ynis grabbed them by their collar and lifted them halfway up. Guin managed a low squeaking sound, which grew louder as a stream of air rushed in. Ynis held them against her breastplate. Her wide eyes bored into Guin's with gentle heat.

"Let it out slow, baby," Ynis said in a trembling voice. Air whistled out of Guin's chest, which then convulsed as it expanded. At last, they were able to take in a noisy breath. Their lungs burned with sweet relief. "Yes, yes, yes, you're doing great. Just keep breathing, just like that."

The pain in their lungs was soon surpassed by the spot of searing fire in their back and the pounding of their head, which lolled back until Ynis caught it with a sure hand.

"I got you, girl," Ynis cooed, tears streaking down her trembling, smiling face. Guin's mouth stretched toward a smile as their eyes rolled slowly back. They looked up in a daze at the patch of sky between the walls of the canyon. For a moment before they passed out, they could have sworn a pair of hazel eyes glinted down at them from above.

SEVEN

Ynis stood guard over Guin's sleeping form. She'd hauled them downstream far enough to get out of the canyon, weeping from the pain as she shouldered Guin, mashing her white-hot wound the whole way down. She'd sprinkled the last few drops of antiseptic on, for what good it would do at this point beyond making the pain so blinding she almost passed out. She shivered despite the warm autumn sun. The cool night was going to be unbearable with all this rock to drain what little warmth her body was still capable of producing.

Guin's breathing was regular and strong, thank all the gods Ynis didn't believe in. Maybe there was an Angel watching over them after all. The back of their head was bruised and a little swollen, but not enough for serious concern; their coif and padding had done their job. The back injury was more a cause for worry. They'd taken a pretty big hit from the rock, possibly saving her life. They groaned, eyes still closed, as Ynis wrestled their mail shirt off to get a better look. A purplish-blue bruise stretched across half their back. It was already beginning to swell, which couldn't be a good sign.

Guin stirred with a whine as she poked gently around the edge of the bruise. This might be serious or it might just be ugly; Ynis was no medic. She pulled their shirt back down gingerly, her fingers brushing the taut muscles of Guin's back.

"How bad is it?" Guin croaked, turning their head halfway to look up at Ynis.

"I don't think anything's broken. Can you wiggle your fingers and toes?" Ynis' heart warmed with relief as Guin made two fists and rotated their feet slowly.

"Where are we?" Guin looked around, dazed, face scrunching in pain as they rolled onto their stomach and pushed up to an awkward crouch.

"A couple hundred yards downstream, just outside the canyon mouth."

Guin let out a long, loud sigh as they pushed back onto their haunches, hands pressed into their knees. They straightened up most of the way, gasping for breath. "How in the Upside Down did I get here?"

Ynis looked down at her hands, unable to meet Guin's gaze for the moment. "I carried you."

"You—how?" Guin's eyes fixed on Ynis' shoulder, which throbbed with hot agony.

"I did what any soldier would do."

Guin's eyes softened as they met Ynis'. "Thank you."

Ynis waved off the thanks, though it felt oddly good to hear it said with such sincerity. "Thank me by getting to your feet. We can't camp here, but there's some decent cover a little farther down. I can help—"

Guin pushed up, body shuddering with the effort. They stood, only slightly hunched, their breath a forced whine. "Fuck," they said through gritted teeth. "Sorry."

Ynis cracked a smile. "You've heard how I curse when I'm in pain. You're a damned angel if all you say is one little 'fuck.'"

Guin winced a smile as they took a hesitant step. They held their body at a strange angle, as if to compensate for the injury, but it didn't appear to be helping.

"Here." Ynis offered her arm, which Guin gripped tightly as they took a step, then another. On their third step, they let out a sudden wail and slumped into Ynis' arms. She shuffled her feet to better support them without overusing her bad shoulder. They were heavy, and she was sweating in her full armor and padding.

"Shh-shh-shh." Ynis held Guin tight as their breathing settled with a shudder. Tears streaked down the dust on their cheek. "I've got you. Take your time." In truth, they needed to get moving, as Ynis was struggling to hold Guin upright.

"Okay," Guin breathed, holding Ynis' hip to push themself back up to standing. "Okay." After a couple of deep breaths, they took a tentative step forward. They paused, breathing deeply again, and took another. And another.

It was slow, hot going. When the sun dipped behind a passing cloud, a chill swept over Ynis' body. By the time they reached the trio of spindly cedar trees that were the closest thing she could see to shelter, she was drenched in sweat and her throat was parched.

"Water," Guin croaked, leaning against a tree, arms flopped at their sides. Ynis uncorked Guin's skin and lifted it to their lips. She poured in a few gentle drops, then a little more. Soon, Guin's hand rose to take the waterskin. They gripped Ynis' hand for a moment as their eyes rose to meet hers. "Thank you," they said softly.

"Don't mention it." Ynis took a drink from her own skin, which was lukewarm and stale, with the metallic tang of the purifying tab as an added bonus. She knew she had to choke down all of it to stay hydrated, despite the awful taste.

"We need to refill before night." Guin gestured with their chin; the stream was only twenty yards away, fully exposed. "I've got three tabs left. You?"

"Same." The rule of thumb was one waterskin per day minimum on mission, more in periods of high activity. That didn't leave much room for error. The water in streams like this could carry uncurable bugs that would eat a person alive over the course of months, but the tabs were expensive, so they were rationed precisely. "Let's hope your Angel shows up on schedule tomorrow night."

Guin turned to the mountain, a frown growing on their lips. "I think we're supposed to be higher up." They gestured vaguely upward. "Just above the canyon, I think."

"And you...saw this? In your vision?"

Guin nodded. Ynis couldn't say why she believed Guin; it was the sort of thing she'd always found ridiculous, people living their lives according to the dictates of imaginary sky beings. If it wasn't the Grey Angel, it was the Exalted Mother, or the Voice of the Wind, or the Sun-Queen. People telling themselves stories instead of figuring it all out for themselves. But maybe that's what religion was, in the end; figuring life out by telling stories. Guin's story was one she desperately needed to hear.

"I know it sounds crazy, I just—"

"It doesn't." Ynis put a hand on Guin's shoulder, looking into their soft, hopeful eyes. "I believe you. And if you believe in Her, so do I."

"I don't believe." Guin's eyes hardened as they gripped Ynis' bicep. "I *know*."

Ynis' eyes fluttered closed as they fought the sudden urge to kiss Guin. She'd never thought of them like that before, other than in the usual way, in stray moments in her dark bedroom at night. But that was true of many women—*people,* she reminded herself. Ynis was as omnivorous in her fantasies as she was choosy in real life.

This was different.

Ynis released Guin and took half a step back, holding onto a tree for support as she grew slightly woozy. Guin moved to put a hand beneath her free arm, but Ynis waved them off.

"I'm fine, I just...the sun took it out of me a bit." Her sweat-drenched hair was like strands of ice across her head and neck. She wrenched the helmet off, letting Guin take it as she flipped her coif and padding back and let the fresh air wash over her head and into her lungs. If the geller wanted to come for her now, she'd take her chances.

"You sit. I'll get the water." Guin set Ynis' helmet in a patch of sun, badly hiding a wince as she stood back up.

"Guin, don't be ridiculous, you should rest." Ynis planted her hands to push up, then stopped at Guin's outstretched palm.

"I need to move, or it'll freeze up." They eyed the stream, then squinted up toward the canyon. "Might want to keep your crossbow handy, just in case."

A cold front moved in by late afternoon, though thankfully the grey clouds seemed to be keeping to the north. They'd managed to set up the tarp to shelter them from the worst of the wind, but the cold had sunk into Ynis' bones. She had to actively work to keep her teeth from chattering. They made what fire they could, and Ynis rotated to keep warm as Guin helped remove her armor. They seemed to avert their eyes as they pulled off her hauberk, leaving her shivering in padding and underthings only.

"Go ahead." Guin gestured toward her sleep pocket, still rolled up next to her pack. "I'll scout the perimeter real quick while you get ready. Maybe I can scrounge up another few branches while I'm at it." They moved stiffly but remained on two feet, which was more than Ynis could say for herself as she crawled between the layers. She curled in on herself in the hopes of generating some warmth. She startled at the cracking of branches, then settled as she realized it was just Guin getting firewood.

The cedar fronds beneath her sleep pocket blunted the rocks and roots a little, but the cold wormed its way through. Her fingers and feet were like icicles. Even her core felt the heat draining from it moment by moment. The only part of her that wasn't cold was where the wound's ugly heat throbbed. Spikes of hot pain flashed through her shoulder and neck every time sleep approached.

She was vaguely aware of Guin's presence, their vigilance shielding her like an iron bulwark. Nothing would reach her without going through them. The cold was not deterred by Guin's vigil, however; soon Ynis began shivering. She fought to stop it, but she was so weak, so cold. Her body ached from the effort; her mind grew hazy, thoughts twisting around each other like seaworms.

An image rose in her mind of a shadowy figure descending on her, bringing darkness with it. Light returned as it spoke, *She* spoke, words of comfort Ynis could not understand. The Angel lay down behind Ynis, cradling her in Her arms, bringing warmth and hope to her delirium. She murmured in Ynis' ear, words like birdsong echoing across the mountain. Ynis' body warmed with the closeness. The

Angel's words came clear at last, a whisper across the void,
Her breath hot in Ynis' ear.

"I will never let anything happen to you."

EIGHT

Guin sought no visions of the Angel that night.

One lay in their arms, finally warm and still, snoring—sometimes gently, and sometimes less so. Guin tried to remove their hand from between Ynis' breasts, where she had pulled it, but she let out a little moan in her sleep and clutched tighter, trapping them in place. It felt unchivalrous, holding her so closely with her in this delirious state. It felt doubly unchivalrous of Guin's cock to strain against Ynis' backside, but they were helpless against the soft, muscled heat of her body. It was a physical reaction, nothing more; if Ynis noticed in her delirium, surely, she couldn't hold it against them.

The mountain was silent save for the whisper of wind in the treetops and the dwindling crackle of the fire. Guin kept their ears alert for any other sound; the geller might be stealthy enough to try to sneak up on them, but the click of those claws never came, and no guttural snarls pierced the quiet. Guin's back ached from staying in the same position all night as much as from the bruise, but they would have endured all the torments of the Upside Down if it meant spending just a few more moments with Ynis in their arms.

Dawn came too soon, dim and grey under a curtain of tumultuous clouds. Guin extricated themself from Ynis' warmth and rebuilt a meager fire, moving stiffly and with significant pain, but at least they could move. They'd expected worse. Ynis' face was uncharacteristically ashen, her lips chapped and pale. She hovered over the fire, staring into it with hollow eyes. She'd looked away as Guin checked her wound, which they immediately wished they hadn't done. The wound had filled with pus, with angry red streaks leading away from it like hungry vines. Ynis did not ask how it looked, and Guin was only too happy not to mention it.

They both knew what was at stake. Ynis had made her choice.

Guin could only hope it wouldn't kill her.

"My knee is swollen and stiff, too." Ynis pulled out a tin of lip tint and spread it with a practiced gesture, touching it up in the tin's mirror and wiping a grey smudge off her cheek.

"But at least you'll look pretty for the geller."

Ynis shot Guin an inscrutable look. "It's called moisturizing. You should try it." She held out the tin with fingers still perfectly manicured, despite all they'd been through.

Guin couldn't deny their lips were rather cracked. "Thanks." They smeared a dab on their finger and spread it across their lips, awakening their nose with a whiff of citrus and honeyblossom. As they pressed their lips together to seal it, their eyes drifted to the soft curve of Ynis' lips, the little divot in the center, the faint line of scar leading across her cheek, beckoning the eye toward her ear and the stray curls that hovered around it, having escaped her braid—

"Is there something..." Ynis touched her ear, snapping Guin from their spell.

"Nothing, sorry, just...just tired."

"You seemed to sleep all right last night, judging from your snoring." Ynis' wink sent Guin into a spiral of embarrassment and confoundment. They hadn't slept a wink. They were sure of it.

"That's...that's my line," they managed.

"Touché." Ynis raised her hands in surrender. Her smile brought color to her face for a moment, and no doubt to Guin's, too, and that seemed to be the end of it. Soldiers didn't talk about the awkwardness of sleeping in the same pocket against the cold. They just made jokes about it and pretended like it was nothing. Which it was. Nothing.

Nothing was going to happen between them and Ynis. She was their mena, and such relations were strictly against Haemene protocol. Not that there was any chance to begin with; Ynis was a lesbian, and Guin was...whatever they were, but definitely not what Ynis was into. Though she never spoke of it, everyone knew of her conquests. They were all women, each one more beautiful than the last. Guin didn't stand a chance.

Especially not if Ynis died of infection up here on the mountain. Yet neither of them spoke of going back. They were united in purpose, however foolish.

The Angel would come to them this night.

They had to be ready.

The trek around the canyons would have been arduous in any case, but in their condition, it was torture. Ynis'

fever had returned, and she walked with an ever-more-pronounced limp. But she was a soldier before all else, and she bore her pain in silence. Guin's back ached all the time. At odd moments, a sharp pain would bring them to a halt, and on one occasion, to their knees. Something was wrong. The way back would be difficult if not impossible, but none of that seemed to matter.

They trekked ever upward, stopping to rest several times before they finally stood above the canyon under a clearing sky. They refilled their waterskins, using another precious tab, bringing them one day closer to dehydration or worse. Guin had wondered if maybe the water would be better this high up, but there were still a few animal tracks, from goats mostly. The water would not be safe.

After a pathetic lunch of one half-stick of jerky and one half of a hardcake each, they continued upward. There were no game trails at this point, at least none that led uphill. The goats seemed to move side to side, crossing the stream periodically in shallow places.

They came upon an unexpected grove of silverbarks around a natural pool in the stream in late afternoon. Ynis shucked her pack and slumped against a tree, her eyes already closed in a soldier's rest. Guin glanced up toward the peak, which they could reach the next day if they kept climbing. A set of dark openings yawned out of the stone, vaguely resembling a skeletal face, but for the extra hole off to the left. You couldn't see them from lower down, but up here, it was obvious why it was called Wicked Peak.

"Go shoot us a goat," Ynis mumbled, eyes still closed, mouth tilting toward a faint smile.

"How about some nice roast geller?"

Ynis convulsed with sudden laughter, which turned into a cough that nearly had her retching. "I need to eat something, or I'll throw up, but if I eat something, I'm afraid I'll throw up."

"They say silverbark tea is good for nausea." Guin picked at the bark of a nearby tree. It peeled off easily beneath their fingernails, like paper. "I've never made it, though."

"Boiling might be good enough for the water up here."

Guin wasn't as sure, but with the number of tabs they had left, it seemed like a decent risk. They gathered wood for a fire and got it started while Ynis dozed against the tree. Even in this pitiful state, she was beautiful: strong cheeks, full lips, a neck full of grace and strength. She obviously took feminizing philters, as evidenced by her breasts and hips, and her behind—Guin turned away as the memory of lying next to Ynis rose in their mind, though it wasn't like she could see them blush, being asleep. It just felt wrong to look at her without her knowledge.

Guin busied themself boiling water for the tea in the big steel mug, using the long, detachable handle to set it in the fire. They'd picked it up at a yardware sale on a whim, and it was consistently the most useful part of their kit. They peeled off a good handful of bark, which had a vivid, almost citrusy aroma when crushed. They boiled it until the tea took color, then set it aside on a rock to steep. They did another search of the grove, which was about twice the size of a cottage, with silverbarks dipping their roots all around the pool at its center. On a flat rock at the water's edge were a number of stones, some of them stacked three and four high. Climbers' markers. Guin scrounged on the ground until they found two pebbles flat enough to support another in case they ever came back.

They placed them side by side on the rock. By tradition, Ynis should place her own, but Guin doubted she cared about that sort of thing. They placed one atop the other for a moment, to see if it would hold, which of course it did, gravity being inescapable. They put them side by side again as they pictured themself and Ynis climbing this mountain again, not as soldiers in peril but as lovers on holiday. They would bathe in this pool, as no doubt many had done before, bodies prickling from the cold. Giggling, tickling each other as they dried off, huddling together in a sleep pocket made for two.

"This really is a lovely spot." Ynis' voice nearly startled Guin into the water. "We should come here on holiday sometime. Add another pebble. Though technically," she continued, reaching to pick up one of the pebbles and set it back down, "it only counts if I set it there myself."

"Which you now have," Guin managed, wondering how Ynis was even on two feet, let alone cracking jokes. Unless she'd read Guin's mind, which was impossible. "Welcome to the exclusive Wicked Peak society, member number..." They counted the stones with their eyes. "Seventeen."

"Sixteen, I should think, since I arrived first."

Guin had rarely seen Ynis like this, unguarded, not in command. "I feel obligated to object on the grounds that you only reached the *grove* first. It was I who first reached the board."

"Am I going to have to pull rank on you, soldier?"

Guin's mind flashed with images that sent a rush of blood to their face. *Gods, please.* "I withdraw my objection, Number Sixteen."

Ynis shouldered them gently, smiling into the leaf-dappled pool. "No sign of..."

Guin shook their head. "Not a trace."

"Maybe it's afraid of the Angel."

Guin pondered. If the Grey Angel were truly here on this peak, the geller might well be aware of Her and know to avoid Her territory. But something wasn't right, something slippery and dim that eluded their attempts to pin it down. "I don't think so, but don't ask me why."

"Can I ask you *how* you know not to think so? Is that allowed?"

Guin heaved a chuckle, poking a stick they'd been playing with into the pool. "If I knew, I would tell you."

"If you say so." Ynis stepped back and pulled her crossbow around front, though her posture did not suggest an immediate threat. "At any rate, we need to keep our eyes open."

"And our minds," Guin murmured to themself.

"I'm cold," Ynis whined from her sleep pocket as Guin stood watch by the small fire.

"Is your fever back?" Guin wasn't sure how she'd shaken it; her wound was bad enough that it might require surgery when she got back to cut out the infected tissue, and they were all out of antiseptic.

"No," she said in a small voice that tore at Guin's heart. "Just cold."

Guin stared into the dark forest, painted with flecks of silver and grey from the moonlight. Their mena was asking them to share her bed, despite the threat of the geller. Despite the impending arrival of the Angel, which felt more and more like a fantasy with each passing moment. They took their own sleep pocket, unfolded it, and laid it over Ynis' rounded form, tucking it in gently around the edges.

"Fine, be that way," Ynis said with a little pout as Guin was tucking in the edge around her shoulder.

"Mena, someone has to stand watch."

"No one stood watch last night."

Guin gazed into the darkness, their soldier mind battling their besotted heart and losing badly. "If you ordered me to lie down, I could not refuse."

Ynis turned on her side away from Guin. "I would never order you to do something so reckless."

Guin stood with fists clenched, unsure how to take Ynis' words or her tone. They simply had no framework to have this conversation with their leader. They added a branch to the fire to stall for time. Ynis did not stir, and Guin remained where they were, locked in a game of self-doubt and frustration. In time, Ynis' breathing steadied, judging by the regular rise and fall of the sleep pockets. Not long after, a whistling snore sounded, barely audible above the creek's gurgling song.

If they'd made a different choice, Guin would be cradling Ynis in their arms, pressed against her soft strength, hand cradled in the warmth between her breasts. Their resolve hardened as they thought of the other Angel that might visit tonight. The ring of trees around the pool left a circular patch of sky open. The bright quarter moon was just cresting the canopy, rising above the peak's crooked top. It was almost in the position they'd seen in their vision, but no silver-limned shadow marred its bright face. Guin's eyes dropped to the forest beyond the pool, a landscape of dappled shadow that flowed and shifted from the breeze in the treetops.

The movement was confusing to the eye, unpredictable, with swaths of darkness seeming to creep ever closer before dissipating into the pattern. One of these shadows failed to vanish as it approached with sinuous grace. Guin inched their crossbow in the direction of its movements without raising it to take sight; better that the geller think it had surprised them. It disappeared behind a pair of conjoined silverbarks at the water's edge for so long that Guin wondered if they'd imagined it. Why was it here? Why did it keep coming after them? Why did it not just flee into the hills until they were gone?

A cloud passed over the moon, dimming the shadows further. Guin sensed movement but could no longer be sure where the geller was. They trained their crossbow on the darkness where it had disappeared. Should they wake Ynis and tip their hand? They leaned down to pick up the branch of dried leaves they'd kept by the fire for the occasion, crossbow aimed between a pair of ghostly white trunks where the geller seemed most likely to appear.

The shadow between the trees grew darker. Guin shoved the branch into the fire. The dead leaves flared in an instant, and Guin swung the branch toward the gap. The geller hissed, showing every one of its sharp teeth and covering its eyes with its clawed hands.

Ynis rolled awkwardly out of her covers and scrambled for her broadsword. Guin let out a roar and leapt forward, shoving the burning branch toward the creature. It leapt back with a sky-splitting screech but quickly recovered as the flames died down, skittering closer with teeth bared. Guin poked it, hoping to make it jump back, but it deflected the blow with its shoulder and broke the branch against the tree.

Guin raised their crossbow too late; the geller was already on them, forcing them to the ground as it raked at their stomach with its powerful hind legs. Guin's shoulders were pinned, so they did the only thing they could think of and headbutted the creature with all their might. It squealed and rolled off Guin, who sat up, vision spinning and blood trickling down their face.

Ynis closed on the creature. The sound of their battle faded to a distant din. Guin's eyes drifted up to starry blue-black sky, the quarter moon radiant, save for an odd shadow in its center. Their eyes widened as the shadow grew and grew, taking on a familiar shape: wings, curves, and dark, piercing eyes. She flapped Her wings furiously to slow Her descent, but She was coming in too fast, there was no way She could stop herself—

She landed with a great splash, sending Her sprawling face-first in the pool, wings spread wide like giant dead leaves. The geller screamed and leapt into the water, with Ynis hot on its heels. The pool was only waist-deep, and the geller swam while Ynis waded, so the creature reached Her first. It rolled Her onto Her back with gentle movements, then turned to bare its fangs at Ynis as the Angel stood behind it. She snapped Her wings wide, shedding water in a silvery explosion in the moonlight.

Ynis' sword dropped into the pool. She fell to her knees in the water, which came up to her chest, and stared up, wide-eyed, at the being before them. Guin found themself kneeling as well, hands clapped to their chest, eyes streaming like the water sluicing down the Angel's feathers.

The Angel blinked slowly and gave Ynis a single nod. Her wings flicked upward along the inside of Her arms and sides and nearly vanished into Her downy coat. She put a hand on the geller's shoulder; it shrank down like a dog at heel, gazing up at Her with adoration. At last, She turned Her face toward Guin, who bathed in Her radiance. Her eyes were gentle and kind, with melancholy and hope intertwined like shortbean vines.

"I had hoped it would not come to this."

The Angel's voice echoed in the grove, though Her lips did not move. Had the sound only been in Guin's mind? They looked to Ynis, who stared up at Her with rapt adoration. The Angel lifted the geller gently to examine the wound from Guin's crossbow, the bolt's splintered shaft still protruding by several inches. She closed Her eyes, pressing Her fingers against the wound. With a quick but unhurried movement, She gripped the bolt and yanked it out.

A jet of blood shot off into the pool, silvery-black in the moonlight. The geller's squeal lasted but a moment; then She stuck a finger into the wound, stopping the flow of blood and calming the beast with a flurry of low, soft sounds, almost like an owl. The geller looked up at Her, eyes slitted. She made a strange face, almost like She was going to spit.

And then She did, pursing Her lips and releasing a glistening string onto the injury. She quickly pressed her finger atop the ensalivated wound. The geller closed its eyes and made a kind of purr, which the Angel repeated, stirring Guin in new and indescribable ways. She turned Her head toward Guin, still making the purring sound, buttery and warm. Guin's heart stuttered as she blinked, then turned to Ynis, who still knelt chest-deep in the frigid pool.

"Come. Let's warm up by the fire. We have much to discuss."

NINE

Ynis eyed the geller, which hovered just behind the Angel. It watched with curiosity mixed with fear as She tended to Ynis' wounds. Now that Ynis could get a proper look at it, she saw that the fur on its back was intermixed with feathers. Two knobs rose near its shoulder blades, no doubt the beginnings of its wings. Ynis' wound went numb, tension releasing from her shoulder as a cool, tingly sensation crept in. She glanced up to see the Angel pulling the remains of a strand of saliva back between Her lips.

It should have been shocking to have a winged woman-beast-god spitting on her infected wound, but it seemed like the most natural thing in the world. It was euphoric, and not just from having the pain erased. She felt refreshed, made new in a way she'd only ever felt in the flower house after she'd been Shaped. She'd often wondered what manner of science or magic the healers used to make her who she was meant to be. They kept the secrets of their practice close; rumors abounded, but no one knew for sure. The healers weren't Angelites, she didn't think. Perhaps this came from the same source or used the same principles.

"I can cure your blood infection in the same manner if you like." The Angel spoke with words now, unlike before, when Her thoughts had filled Ynis' mind like the heat from a fire. Her voice was rich and dusky, Her expression frank and kind. Ynis nodded, still uncertain if she could form words worthy of Her ears. "I'm going to release saliva into your mouth. Just swallow it as you would any medicine."

Ynis nodded again, heat rising in her cheeks as the Angel closed Her eyes and pursed Her lips. She opened Her eyes and cupped the back of Ynis' head. Ynis lay her head back, staring up into Her steady gaze. The Angel blinked and released a strand of viscous saliva into Ynis' waiting mouth. It tasted of seaweed and honey, warming her tongue as it slid down toward her throat. The Angel lifted Ynis' head as She lowered to meet her mouth and released a final burst in a hot, wet kiss.

Ynis gave a start as their lips parted. She swallowed the slimy mass, savoring the sweet and salty aftertaste.

"Your fever should dissipate by morning." The Angel slowly withdrew Her hand, and Ynis stood, unsteadily at first.

"Thank you, gods, I—" Ynis paused, shaking her head. What had just happened? "I'm sorry, I...I'm Ynis, and this is Guin. We were sent by the Queendom to...hunt the..." She gestured toward the creature, which was studying her as she spoke, though it didn't seem to understand. "We call them geller. I don't...are they...are you?" It was hard, speaking to the most beautiful woman she had ever seen, who had just spit in her mouth and kissed her, who was also apparently some version of the beasts Ynis had slaughtered by the score.

The Angel closed Her eyes for a long moment and sighed. "Few make it to adulthood, due to the...unruly nature of our adolescence." She reached an arm back and scratched the geller behind the ear. It wrapped its arms around Her middle, leaning its head against Her side. "It's why we bring them here."

"Here, as in, the mountains?"

She blinked a smile. "Here, as in, to your world." She gestured around Her, fingers tipped with much shorter claws than the geller's. Or perhaps they were retractable?

Her teeth were much like human teeth, but with longer canines and perhaps a few more sharp teeth on either side. "We choose mountains for the privacy, and also to reduce the loss to your kind and ours, though we know that is always a risk. Our kind develop so quickly—too quickly." She shook Her head, sorrow etched into Her face, which was covered in tiny feathers, except around Her mouth and eyes.

"The onset of puberty, which happens much earlier in our kind than in yours, causes a kind of psychosis, where we do not know friend from foe, human from beast." Her dark eyes were heavy with a regret that Ynis felt in her heart, as if it were her own. "By tradition and law, we must bring them here; those who survive return with us. The rest we mourn."

No one spoke as the Angel's words sank in. Grief emanated from Her in waves, echoing through Ynis' heart. The geller before them was the only one who'd survived. She was mourning Her dead children, which Ynis and Guin might well have killed. Ynis absently took Guin's hand and pulled them closer. A quick glance showed Guin felt it too, probably more so, given their connection to the Angel.

"You said 'we' because..." Guin released Ynis' hand, gesturing toward the mountains in the distance. "There are others like you." Their voice fell in disappointment as they spoke.

"Many," She said, "though we don't reproduce nearly as often as you. The last time I was here..." She gestured toward the valley below and the Queendom beyond. "This land was largely unoccupied."

Guin turned to Ynis, brow furrowed. "Who was here before the Queendom?"

Ynis shook her head, trying to remember her history. "Nomadic peoples...the Iaur, Iori, yes that's it! The ones with the forest sleds." She recalled a drawing in a textbook of a narrow dog-sleigh whose runners were wrapped in furs of some kind, which would be greased to ease its passage along their trails.

Guin nodded, then turned back to the Angel. "So, it's been more than a hundred and twenty years since you were here?"

"In your world, apparently. In mine, it has been ten. Time is not a constant between worlds. There have surely been others who have come since that wave; there are always some who gestate outside of the pattern."

A smile bloomed on Guin's face as they gripped Ynis' shoulders. They spoke in a strange voice, as if reciting a saintly poem. *"Once every generation, there will come a great blossoming."* They gestured back toward the Angel.

"Our religion tells us that in such periods, many will be visited in a short time. Does that mean there are others here right now, on other mountains?"

She nodded, eyes closing softly for a moment. "Calling to other progenitors, all throughout your world."

Ynis and Guin exchanged a confused glance. "Progenitors?" Ynis asked.

The Angel's smile dissolved Ynis' concern. "We search open minds to choose partners to help us conceive." Her hand on Ynis' shoulder melted away any resistance she might have had. When She released her and took Guin's shoulders in Her hands, Ynis' stomach twisted with something between jealousy and desire. "I searched a thousand minds to find you, Guin. You are the most beautiful soul I have encountered." She put a finger under Guin's chin, which lifted toward Her face, half flame, half shadow in the firelight. "A flower among grass. An ocean among ponds." Guin's lips parted as the Angel dipped closer, setting Ynis' mouth salivating and her heart racing in her chest. "A woman worth crossing worlds for."

Guin's eyes flew wide, then fluttered closed as the Angel kissed her, holding her chin aloft with one claw-tipped finger. The signs of Guin's arousal were unmistakable, and a warmth spread through Ynis at the sight of her kissing the Angel with surprising fervor. Guin gasped audibly when the Angel pulled back, running Her long, slender tongue over Her sharp teeth.

"So eager." She released Guin's chin with a slow flourish. "I feel the same." As She looked Guin up and down, it seemed Her eyes lingered on the bulge in her trousers. *Their* trousers, Ynis reminded herself. But hadn't the Angel called— "However, there are protocols that must be followed, consent and custody to discuss, which in this case may prove complicated."

She turned toward Ynis, full lips quirking into a smile. "You are her partner, yes?"

Ynis shot Guin a panicked look, but Guin was staring down at their hands, cheeks alive with color. "They and I...that is, Guin and I are...soldiers, of the Queendom, as I said, and—"

"You said *they*. Do women in this age not use *she*?"

"They do—we do—it's just that—"

"I'm not a woman," Guin said in a soft voice. Ynis held out her hand, wishing there was something she could do to help.

The Angel looked back at Guin, who struggled to meet Her eyes. "In my time, I've touched minds with quite a few humans, and I've only ever been compatible with women."

"I..." Guin ran a hand down their body as if in display. "I guess I never felt like a man, but I'm not...that is I've never…" They shook their head in frustration. The Angel waited, face open, eyes gentle. "I guess I never felt…worthy of womanhood, is how I would put it."

The Angel raised Her eyebrows. "Conceptions of these things do change over time, but can humans in your society not live as a gender different from the one presumed at their birth?"

Guin stared back down at their hands, and Ynis stifled a nervous laugh that tried to bubble up as she spoke. "We can and do. I am such a woman. Some call us Chosen women, as opposed to Made women, but I'm not a fan of the terms; not everyone sees it as a choice."

"But it can be?"

"Yes, of course. In the Queendom, anyway. It's getting harder in the Kingdom, from what I've heard."

"Forgive the insensitivity of my questions. Things have changed since I was last here."

"It's okay," Guin said in a tremulous voice. "I think…for You, anyway, and for Ynis, if she likes," at which point they cast a weak smile at Ynis, "I'd like you to call me she."

"As she wishes." The Angel bowed Her head toward Guin, then eyed them both. "You should know that your gender, or your sex, in the terms that you see it, does not matter for the ritual. We procreate…differently than humans. And you're both invited to join, if you choose—I can carry the...seed, for lack of a better word, of multiple partners."

Ynis stood, mouth agape, images flashing through her mind of the Angel bearing down on her, down on Guin, Guin on her, bodies intertwined, claws and skin and feathers and teeth. "Yes," she breathed.

The Angel stepped toward Ynis with a wicked smile and raised a soft hand to her cheek. The gentle touch of Her claws sent frissons all along Ynis' spine. "A Chosen woman." Her claws scraped down over Ynis' curved breastplate with a faint metallic grating sound. "A Shaped woman." Her fingers dragged along Ynis' sides down to her hips, nails stuttering over the chainmail, lighting a fire between her legs. "I can't wait to see what's beneath all this finely worked metal."

Ynis stood immobile and breathless as the Angel removed her armor piece by piece, clawed fingers dexterously unbuckling straps and laying the pieces gently on the ground. As Ynis stood in her still-damp tunic and underthings, she shivered, and not only at the Angel's touch and gaze.

"You're cold," She said, flicking Her arms to the sides. Her great grey wings snapped out and spread like a massive umbrella, one curving around Ynis and the other around Guin. "And weary." She pulled them into Her tenebrous warmth, wings enfolding them like a feathered tarp, shielding them from the cold and the fear of the world outside. "And injured." Her lips closed on Ynis' shoulder, tongue laving her wound with icy heat that spread through her body like molten steel filling a form. "We shall rest together. When you are both refreshed, the ritual will begin."

"Do you, Guin, of your own free will and without hesitation, agree to join with me, to give of your life to create new life together?"

Guin breathed, "Yes," her face flushed and serene in the firelight. They stood on either side of the Angel, with their sleep pockets spread out in a bed-sized square beneath them all. They'd rested together, wrapped in the Angel's wings, faces buried in Her downy chest. Ynis wasn't sure if she'd slept; or perhaps she was still asleep and this was a dream. In the presence of such glory, it was hard to care.

"Do you understand that our offspring must live with me in my world, under my care and that of my kind, except during their trials and eventual mating?"

Guin stared into the Angel's dark eyes, biting her lip as she nodded.

"If you have questions, please ask." The Angel glanced at Ynis, then back to Guin.

After a long moment, Guin spoke. "And that could be a hundred and twenty years from now."

The Angel nodded. "Or more. Or much less. Time between worlds is highly unpredictable in that regard." She put Her hand to Guin's cheek. "Given your lifespan, you may never see them, or me, again."

"But I might." Guin's voice was soft, hopeful.

The Angel's mouth curved up into a smile that would have been gentle if not for the fangs. "You might."

Guin swallowed, nodding. "I accept." The Angel's eyes slitted as She lowered Her face for a kiss. Guin rose to meet Her, stoking Ynis' desire. It exploded through her body as the Angel's tongue slithered out into the kiss and Her tail slashed through the air to wrap around Guin's body. The Angel pulled Guin in, nails poking dents into the thin fabric clinging to her muscled behind. A lump formed in Ynis' throat at the realization that she now saw Guin as a woman. She bit her lip as the Angel's fingers slid over Guin's hips, then traced down the line of her bulge, which leapt at the touch, accompanied by Guin's desperate gasp.

Her face grew serious for a moment as She released Guin and turned to Ynis. "And you." Her tail rose delicately, then slunk around Ynis' ankles, stirring hot chills up her legs and through her core. "Do you, Ynis, of your own free will and without hesitation, agree to join with me, to give of your life to create new life together?"

Ynis' heart thumped wetly in her chest. "I do." She watched the Angel's lips, teeth, and agile tongue as She repeated the rest of the words, probably the same ones She'd said to Guin. Something pulled taut in Ynis' chest at the mention of offspring, a possibility she'd written off when she'd gotten Shaped. It was a shame she'd never see them, but as she looked into the Angel's kind, dark eyes, her worries dissipated into the open sky.

Ynis must have said yes to the second question; before she knew it, the Angel's mouth was on hers, tongue flickering along her lips, slipping between her parted teeth, tangling with her own as they kissed, long and slow. Ynis gasped as Her tail wrapped around her waist, then slithered between her legs, long and sinuous, firm but feather-soft. She tried to lower herself against it, but it slipped out from between her legs as the Angel pulled back with a wicked smirk.

"Consent has been given and sealed with a kiss." Her eyes flickered from Ynis to Guin and back again. "Though in this case, since there are three parties, it would seem appropriate for a kiss to be shared among *all* of the participants, unless you'd prefer to keep things...separate?"

"No, I mean yes," Ynis stammered as her heart pounded in her throat. "I mean..." She turned to meet Guin's eyes, glassy and golden in the firelight, "I'd like that. That is, if..." She bit her lip, summoned all her courage, and lifted her tunic over her head, shaking her hair out. Incredibly, the wounded shoulder didn't hurt, though it couldn't have been pretty to look at. She stepped toward Guin, whose eyes bored into hers, as if she were afraid to look at Ynis' breasts.

"Yes," Guin breathed, untucking her shirt and pulling it over her head, exposing a muscled chest with delicate curls of dark hair around each pebbled nipple.

Ten

Guin had long denied herself the pleasure of imagining a kiss with Ynis. In the fantasies she did allow, Guin's lips were always...elsewhere. She'd expected Ynis' lips to be soft, but she was not prepared for their silky texture, their extravagant wetness, or the strength with which they reduced her to a tender mess. Ynis gripped Guin's back as her tongue entered the fray, by turns delicate and commanding. Guin strained against the fabric of her underthings, shame mixing with hot need as Ynis' hands traced up her abdomen and hefted her pectorals.

Guin let out a series of little moans as Ynis kissed her way down Guin's neck to explore her chest with lips and tongue, and now teeth as well. She gasped as Ynis took her nipple in her mouth and sucked on it, grazing it with her teeth as her tongue flicked all around. Ynis moved to the other and lavished it with such attentions Guin nearly lost her mind.

She would have lost more than that had Ynis not pulled back. Ynis bit her lip and gazed up at the Angel, who watched with greedy eyes. Ynis shifted back as the Angel stepped toward Guin, eyes roaming from her lips down her chest to the mortifying bulge in her pants.

"May I?" She asked, claws hovering near the tie on Guin's underpants. Guin gulped and nodded, breathing in through her nose, out through her mouth, certain she'd lose it at the slightest touch. The Angel's claws teased apart the knot, then slipped inside her waistband. The gentle scratching on Guin's skin sent frissons of need deep into her belly. The Angel carefully pulled the pants open in front until Guin's cock popped out. Blood rushed to Guin's face as doubt filled her heart. The Angel was only compatible with women, and she was not—

All thought left Guin's mind as a coil of feathery tail snaked between her legs from behind and wrapped itself around her length, sending her into a spiral from which there could be no escape. "Wait," the Angel whispered into her ear. "The road is long. Much will be asked of you before this night is over."

Guin nodded, inching back from the brink. The tail released her cock, slithered back between her legs, and wrapped itself tightly around her waist, pulling her in. *Her* cock. *Her* waist. Guin had never dared think of herself that way, but with Her, it seemed so natural. The Angel's breasts pressed against Guin's chest, warm and downy-soft. Guin's cock pulsed against a patch of fine, damp feathers between Her legs.

The Angel held Guin's waist with Her tail as they kissed. Her hands roamed over every inch of Guin's body, claws skittering across her goose-pimpled skin, leaving a trail of fire in their wake. She plundered Guin's mouth, exploring and sucking and nibbling. Her extravagantly long tongue seemed to wrap around and around Guin's. The sharp points of Her claws dug into Guin's wrist as She took Guin's hand and guided it between Her legs.

What Guin found there was a silky wet slit nestled among fine feathers. She traced delicate lines up and down; the Angel's breath caught as Guin's fingers found a hard nub near the front, impossibly large for a clit. Guin circled it with her fingertips, then eased off when the Angel twitched, gasping. She slid her fingers down the sides of the nub, which was growing, extending like a cock. The Angel's tongue filled Guin's mouth as she slid her fingers all the way to the base and squeezed gently.

Two fingers slipped in, and a third. Just inside Her wet, hot vessel was a rough patch, as on any woman, only it was thicker, with a ropelike shape extending deep within. Guin stroked it, deeper with each pass, until her fingers hit their limit and the Angel grunted with pleasure. Guin gripped Her tight within and used her thumb to caress the base of Her shaft, which was fully erect now, pressed hot and wet against Guin's stomach.

The Angel broke away from her, eyes dark and golden in the firelight, lips kiss-plumped and wet. She flashed a wicked glance at Ynis, then fixed it on Guin. The Angel palmed the top of Guin's head, Her claws pricking harder now, and pushed her down to her knees. Guin gripped the Angel's taut, feathered backside and nosed in, inhaling Her musky aroma, like cherries over-soaked in brandy. She lay tiny kisses over the head of Her slick shaft, followed by licks, gentle at first, then harder. She flicked around the hole at the center, which widened, allowing her to stick her tongue all the way in. The Angel let out an odd mewling noise, like a bush cat in heat.

Guin released Her shaft and kissed her way down along its wet, throbbing length until she reached the now-widened slit with its myriad folds. She breathed in Her musk, then went to work with her tongue, tracing delicate patterns all around while her fingers twiddled the lower end of Her entrance. The Angel's mewling grew into a deep growl, and Her claws tightened around the back of Guin's head, steering her in deeper. Guin took a deep breath and dove in, now in her element once again.

She knew how to make a woman come. Based on the frequency and pitch of the Angel's sounds, She was well on Her way. Just as Guin had moved her fingers back into the game and was teasing the base of the Angel's clit-cock with her tongue, the Angel's clawed hands yanked her back roughly by her hair, and She stared down at her with dark, glistening eyes that burned right through her.

"I'm ready," She said in a husky voice that sent shivers through Guin's body. Those shivers turned to lightning as the Angel grabbed Guin by the shoulders and lay her down on her back like a ragdoll.

Guin glanced at Ynis for a moment and saw her gripping one breast, her other hand between her legs. The Angel straddled Guin. Darkness followed with a snapping sound like an umbrella being unfurled as Her wings overspread them both in a dome of warmth and shadow.

The rest happened as if in a dream. The Angel spoke in her mind, like in the visions, even as She gripped Guin's cock firmly. *This may seem strange, but it should feel good.* Something rubbed against Guin's throbbing tip, something wet and warm—the Angel's clit-cock, Guin realized, only it was opening, pulling her in. The Angel's face was bathed in shadow, mouth set in a toothy rictus of concentration. Her downy breasts dangled above Guin's chest. Her dark nipples glowed orange-yellow in a stripe of firelight that slipped past Her wings. The Angel grunted as She pulled Guin all the way inside Her, tighter at first than any woman she'd been with, so hot and slick Guin knew she wouldn't last much longer.

"Breathe with me." The Angel's mind-voice was soft and oddly desperate, as if She were trying to hold back, too. *"Stay with me."* Her warm, almost fuzzy breasts pressed against Guin's chest as Her lips found Guin's, hungry and languid. As Her tongue slithered in, Guin seized it in her lips, sucking, flicking it with her own even as it coiled and uncoiled like a frenetic snake. Guin gasped as a pulse shot through her cock, and another; the Angel's muscles hardened and Her claws sank into Guin's shoulders, surely drawing blood this time. The pain brought her back from the brink, but not for long.

The Angel moved atop her with the strength of a wild beast and the tenderness of a butterfly sipping nectar from a flower. It was like being fucked for the first time; all she could do was hold on as the Angel plied her with movements quick and slow, gentle and dominating. Guin had always dreamed of being fucked as a woman, though she'd had to settle for receiving, given the parts she'd been born with. Whatever she'd imagined late at night with her hands under the covers in the barracks, trying not to move too much or make a sound—it was nothing compared to the wave of sensation rushing over her.

The Angel's voice echoed in her mind, but it wasn't words; it was a song of some kind, like an elaborate bird call, trilling in time with the shuddering pulses of Her body. The song rose in pitch as Her clit-cock squeezed Guin toward inevitable release. The Angel rocked forward and back, downy breasts slapping Guin's face with each pass. Guin's fingers found the base of Her wings, sturdy, bony knobs perfect for gripping, and held on for dear life as the Angel fucked her into heedless oblivion.

Guin lost her grip as she came, arms flopping down above her head, legs splayed helplessly. The Angel tightened around her, toothy mouth stretched into a tight oval as the last notes of Her song rang out like a high, plaintive lament. Her body froze, trembling, squeezing out every last drop of Guin's pleasure. She expelled Guin with a great muscular wave and a splooshy mess, then collapsed atop her.

The Angel's wings slowly retracted as She lay with her mouth by Guin's ear, breath heavy and hot with exertion, feathers damp with sweat. She pressed tiny kisses along her ear and neck, then lifted herself up enough to stare down into Guin's eyes.

"The ritual was a success," She whispered, lowering Her mouth for a gentle kiss. "You were most accommodating." She lingered in the kiss for a little longer this time. "Thank you," She breathed as She rolled off Guin and lay on Her back with arms splayed above Her. Guin glanced down at Her supine body, Her downy curves, the subtle patterns in the grey of Her feathers, Her serene face. Guin's heart stirred to see Her, the object of her life's dreams and desires, lying next to her in the dark. It didn't feel real, couldn't be—but Guin was lying in a puddle that proved otherwise. She pushed up to sitting and scooted back from the mess. Only then did she notice Ynis, fully naked, limned by the firelight, dark eyes fixed on her.

Guin blinked softly, and Ynis approached, forehead and chest sweaty in the flickering light despite the cool night air. Guin went all hard and soft inside watching her move, the gentle sway of her hips, the bounce and jiggle of her breasts. She lay down next to the Angel, snuggling into Her shoulder and sliding her hand across Her stomach to intertwine with Guin's. Guin settled in across from her, inhaling the musky scent of the Angel's armpit, like that of a woman who's split a hundred logs. Guin's face pressed against the silky softness of Her breast as the Angel hummed and squeezed them closer.

"I must rest," She said, husky voice rumbling through Her chest directly into Guin's ear.

"And once you have rested?" Ynis asked in a voice so innocent it twisted a knot between Guin's legs.

The Angel lifted partway up, the muscles in Her stomach hardening beneath Guin's fingers, and turned to Ynis. "I will perform the ritual with you, and she will watch." She glanced at Guin for a moment, sparking a cascade of desire in her gut, then turned back to Ynis. "You will have...options." She glanced down past their interlaced hands at the slit between Her legs.

"I'll take all of them." Ynis slid a hand around Her neck and pulled Her down for a kiss that lingered as her hand slid down to cup Her breast.

The Angel pulled away from the kiss with a toothy smile, moving Ynis' hand back to Guin's. She let out a chirping sound, like a cat imitating a bird. It was repeated from not far away; the geller—or was it an adolescent Angel?—was keeping watch. She lay Her head back and closed Her eyes.

"After I rest."

Eleven

"What's it like?" Ynis asked into the darkness. They were all awake now, intertwined, breathing together, with the Angel's wings folded over them as a blanket. "Where you're from."

After a long pause, the Angel spoke. "It's a lot lighter, for one thing. Or rather, I am. This world is...heavy." She held out Her hands cupped together, as if weighing the world.

"Are there people? Like, humans?"

"No." The Angel's voice carried a note of sadness, which rose into something like curiosity as She continued. "Although there are some who suggest, sensibly in my opinion, that we...were once like you. Or, rather, we *were* you, and we...changed, over time, after we crossed into our world for the first time. There are many competing theories, scientific and religious, on this very question, but one thing is not in doubt: We require you in order to procreate."

Ynis gazed up at the stars, wondering if one of them was Her world. What it looked like. If it had trees and clouds and a sun. If it was filled with cities of Angels like in the old paintings, all light and wings and decadence, Angels bending each other over a creative variety of objects and animals, riding each other in gardens and ponds. Was there a king, or a queen, or something else entirely? Or perhaps they simply needed no government.

Guin's voice broke the silence. "So, you're just...beings from another world who come here to fuck us every few decades and let your feral kids run wild, hoping they won't kill too many of us in the process?" It was hard to tell how much she was joking.

"How many of our kind have you killed?" The Angel's voice softened the rebuke, but they all fell silent for a long time. Ynis' heart ached with the pain of Her loss, which flowed from Her like lava. Guin's damp fingers squeezed hers gently across the Angel's feathery stomach. No words could undo what they'd done or heal these wounds. They were connected to Her in joy and tragedy, in the making and taking of life.

"I apologize," She said at last, lifting a great weight from Ynis' chest. "That was not...diplomatic. And it's not your fault. You have a duty to protect your kind. If we had known this area was occupied…" She sighed. "Some have advocated for open diplomacy with humans to prevent this from happening, but the risk has been deemed too great. There are always willing partners, thanks to your religion." She turned and kissed Guin's forehead. "But your leaders can be wary of change. Once, long ago…" She trailed off, sighing through Her nose.

"I shouldn't ruin our night with history lessons. By law and tradition, we are not allowed to be seen, or speak with humans, or interact, outside of the ritual. I'm using a…technicality to share as much as I have, since the ritual isn't fully complete in this case until I have joined with Ynis. So, if there's anything else you want to ask, now is the time."

"Whom do you love?" Guin's earnest voice and words stirred Ynis more than they should have. "Where you're from?"

The Angel turned to Guin, who closed her eyes as they kissed. "Many." Her wings retracted as She rolled to face Ynis. "Speaking of which," She said in a low voice, hand sliding over the curve of Ynis' hip, claws dragging lightly, raising hot chills in their path, lips inching closer, "if you're feeling well rested—"

Ynis seized Her neck and kissed Her, long and hard. Her teeth banged against Her fangs as their mouths crushed together. The Angel's tongue was everywhere at once, as were Her hands. She straddled Ynis, sliding Her hands up from her thighs to her hips to cup her breasts, slowly tightening. Her thumbs and forefingers found her nipples and squeezed with the gentlest pressure, claws pricking as the Angel ravished her mouth. Ynis was normally one to lead in situations like this, but when the Angel released her breasts and pinned her down by her biceps, she arched into Her, suddenly so close already, though they had hardly touched.

The Angel rubbed against her, both of them already wet, Ynis' nerves on fire with need. But every time she rose into Her, She lightened the pressure, driving her into a cycle of crests and falls from which there was no escape. Ynis' body throbbed at the softness of Her feathered breasts against Ynis' skin, the hardness of Her growing clit, which stayed wet as it lengthened, like Her now-flowered slit. The Angel slid up and down Ynis' entrance, sparking tremors every time the almost-sharp underside of its head brushed against her clit.

The Angel kissed Her way down her neck, still teasing with Her clit, poking at Ynis' entrance as Her lips found her nipple and sucked it into Her mouth. Ynis arched into

Her as Her long tongue flickered and battered, sharp teeth pressing gently into her skin, then not so gently, turning her into a volcano of molten desire.

"Fuck me," Ynis hissed. She grabbed Her slick clit and pushed the tip inside herself.

The Angel hesitated, concern etched across Her brow. She held Her body rigid, Her hard clit pulsing against Ynis, poised to strike. "Are you sure?"

"Yes," Ynis whispered. She braced herself; she wasn't usually the one to receive, but she didn't usually have a dark Angel from another world pinning her biceps down, either. The Angel's claws dug into Ynis' arms and Her eyes darkened as She pushed inside so slowly it seemed like She was a mile long. Ynis took in a slow breath as She bottomed out, poking her almost uncomfortably deep within.

She was not thick, not at first, anyway. The pressure inside Ynis lessened for a moment, then Her clit began to swell. It became thicker instead of longer, spreading out to stretch and fill Ynis like a rigid balloon. Ynis let out a hoarse cry she was powerless to stop. The Angel closed Her eyes, face tight with concentration, and made a purring sound whose vibrations played Ynis' stretched nerves like a brush-harp.

"Shh, stay with me," She murmured, laying soft kisses on Ynis' lips. "Be with me now. This cannot be rushed."

Ynis accepted the kisses, unable to form words or thoughts as the Angel pulsed inside her in waves that carried Ynis through crest after crest. The Angel breathed hard through Her nose now, releasing Ynis' biceps and sliding Her hands down to knead her breasts. She leaned back, eyes closed as if in prayer. Her lithe body undulated against Ynis, pushing and pulling the knot of Her clit in every direction. Shivers of ecstasy flowed through Ynis' body as She ground against her clit, breathing hoarsely through Her mouth now, swelling inside her, stretching Ynis to her limit and beyond.

The Angel lifted Ynis from within, forcing her hips up as her body spasmed and gushed with pleasure. Warm trickles of blood flowed toward her neck from the gashes Her claws had made around her breasts. The Angel's final shudders ignited a burst of white-hot pleasure that turned Ynis' mind inside out.

A distant cry like a wolf's sounded, ever closer, louder, more desperate, as if caught in a trap. The Angel kissed Ynis, abruptly ending the sound, which Ynis now realized had come from her own mouth, and rode her down to the ground, Her breath hot and heavy in Ynis' ears. Her clit deflated with each pulse, each throb, until at last She slipped out and melted on top of her, sweaty feathers on wet skin atop a soaked sleep pocket.

The Angel rolled to the side, into the waiting arms of Guin, who spooned Her as She lay half atop Ynis. The stars in the sky pulsed in time with the rhythm of the Angel's body, which echoed throughout Ynis' core, bringing little aftershocks of the almost unbearable ecstasy she had endured in Her arms.

The fire had sunk to embers by this point, but the Angel was a furnace. Ynis and Guin wrapped Her up like a pair of wings and soared off to sleep as one.

Guin was stoking the fire when Ynis stirred, still glued to the Angel's downy warmth. Her backside was ice cold, so she rolled over and scooted against the Angel, who put an arm around her with a pouty groan.

"You're cold."

"Not all of us have a coat of feathers to keep us warm."

"And so, you build fires. And, apparently, let my child play with them."

Ynis craned her neck to see the geller drop an armful of branches at Guin's feet, then look up at her expectantly.

"Good girl!" Guin said, as if talking to a dog or a young child. "Go ahead and put them in, one by one, like this."

She demonstrated, and the geller followed suit, glancing back up at Guin for approval. "You're a quick study. Go ahead and do three more." Guin held up three fingers, and the geller put another stick in. Guin beamed at the creature, then turned her smiling face toward Ynis, who had to blink at her radiance. Ynis turned back around with a smile and snuggled into the Angel's warmth.

"What's your name?" she asked after a moment.

"In our language," She began, voice low in Ynis' ear, then said something between a word and a bird call in three syllables. "Here, I prefer Dusk."

"Dusk." Ynis tasted the word as she studied Her sculpted arm, dark grey on top and lighter beneath, soft feathers tightly woven so they felt almost like cat fur. "It suits you."

"You suit me." Dusk took Ynis' ear between Her teeth and squeezed not quite to the point of pain. "I wish I could take you with me. Both of you."

Something sharp lodged in Ynis' chest, and she lay with that pain for a moment. How could she feel this way about someone—some*thing*—she'd just met? "I know you can't, but...can you tell me why?"

Dusk sighed hot into her ear. "It is forbidden for humans to come to our world." She sighed again. "And even if it were not, you could not survive there for long, just as

I cannot live here. Things are...lighter there. You are not built for it."

Ynis puzzled over the description. "How do you mean, lighter?"

Dusk sat up, leaning back on Her elbows, and Ynis sat up with Her, feeling her nakedness suddenly as Guin looked over with poorly disguised interest. Dusk gestured Guin over, and by the time Ynis had wrestled her tunic and pants on, they were seated in a circle on the laid-out sleep pockets.

"Good morning," Dusk said, nodding to Guin. "And to you, of course," She added, turning back to Ynis. "I trust that is still a tradition in your world."

"We usually kiss good morning," Ynis said with a smirk bolder than she felt, stomach roiling as she tangled her fingers with Guin's and pulled her in. Guin's smile melted into something so soft and earnest that Ynis had to kiss her for quite some time, one hand on her tight hip, the other on her muscled chest. "Like that." Ynis turned back to the Ang—to Dusk, feeling brazen despite the blood rushing to her cheeks.

Dusk nodded gravely, studying both their faces for a moment. "It is our first principle to respect the cultures and traditions of your world." She turned to Ynis and slowly closed the short distance between their mouths, angling sideways as She spoke. "No matter what...compli-cations may arise."

Ynis melted into the kiss, into the strong arms now grip-ping her shoulders. The Angel's clawed hands skittered across her tunic on the way down to grip her behind with sharp-pointed tenderness. Heat pooled in her belly as their bodies pressed together, lips and tongues entangled in a heady dance. Her hips swung toward the Angel, suddenly desperate for pressure and friction. The Angel pulled back, licking Her lips with that long, long tongue, and slid Her hands up to press against Ynis' chest.

"I presume coitus isn't a part of your traditional morn-ing greetings." Dusk chucked Ynis' chin with a knuckle, nearly knocking her over, so faint was she from the kiss.

"We could make an exception."

Dusk blinked slowly, as if with regret. "Sadly, time will not permit it. We must return to the peak by tonight, and it is a long way to go in my condition."

"Your...condition?" Guin tugged Her arm. The Angel turned and took Guin's forearms in Her hands. Ynis felt Guin's concern through her expression and shared it.

Dusk sighed. She'd been doing a lot of that this morn-ing. "I mentioned everything feels heavy here. Back home, I can fly." She snapped Her wings out, startling Ynis with the crisp noise. "Here, I can barely glide. I am heavier here. I am not built for this world."

"So going uphill is..."

"Much harder. But I will have fond memories to keep me company along the way." She slid Her hands up Guin's arms to frame her shoulders. Guin's body seemed to go limp as Dusk pulled her in roughly, kissing her with such fervor Ynis started to salivate. "Good morning," She said to Guin as she released her. Ynis took Guin's hand, as she looked none too steady on her feet. Guin blinked thanks as she gave Ynis' fingers a little squeeze.

"So." Dusk rubbed Her hands together. "What's for breakfast?" She let out a set of trilling sounds, a bit like how She'd said Her name. The geller stood on her hind paws and yipped a response, then turned and tore down the path out of sight. "She'll catch me something, which I'm happy to share, of course, though I expect you'd need to cook it."

The smile on Dusk's lips as She watched Her child disappear hit Ynis deep, in a place she'd long ago walled off. She would never know that feeling, never see the fruit of her non-existent womb grow up and become an independent being, maybe have a family of their own someday. She sniffed, turning away to hide the tears that tried to form. Not all women were destined for motherhood. Perhaps it was just as well. She'd never have to know such loss as the Angel had suffered, Her children killed by Guin and Ynis' own hands.

"Fresh meat would be a welcome reprieve from what little we have left." Guin rummaged around in her bag—Ynis smiled wistfully, a twinge in her heart. *Her* bag. It felt so good to think of her that way without second-guessing herself. Why was Ynis getting all emotional about every little thing? It had taken Ynis time to see it, and Guin even longer, but their encounter with Dusk seemed to have helped them both turn the corner. "I don't know if you can eat these, but you're welcome to try. We call them hardcakes. They taste like shit and they're always stale, but they keep you going." Guin broke off a corner and handed it to Dusk, who picked it up delicately between three claws and sniffed it.

She wrinkled her nose, then placed it on her tongue and closed her mouth, crunching thoughtfully. "You're right about the taste, and they certainly aren't fresh, but I can digest this, though I may pay for it later."

They shared the last of their hardcakes, which would mean a long, hungry trip back, but that was a problem for another time. Sitting around the little fire with Guin and Dusk was worth every dreadful bite.

TWELVE

"How do you speak our language, anyway?" Guin asked as they waited for the cliff hog to finish roasting on their meager fire. The geller sat a little farther from the fire, gnawing contentedly on a bloody leg. Dusk had set aside a hearty portion of flesh and entrails for Herself between some leaves as they waited. Guin tried to ignore how revolting it was; cooking fresh meat was probably equally odious to the Angel.

"It is required in school, and returning mothers share the changes they've picked up upon their return. We mostly learn from searching your thoughts; not all humans think in words, but many do."

"And this has been going on for how long now?"

Dusk spread Her clawed fingers wide. "No one knows for sure. There are various legends about how and why, but...beyond our recorded history, at any rate. Our species is...dependent on yours. It seems we lost the ability to safely reproduce on our own eons ago. Pairings between two of our kind often result in miscarriage, stillbirth, or deformed offspring."

"Like horses mated too close to the family line," Ynis remarked.

"That is one theory, and the basis for one of our religions. You are sacred to us. You are essential." Her dark eyes fell almost reverently on Guin's, then flicked to Ynis. "Another theory is that we are a branch of your kind who move between worlds, thanks to a gift from one of our gods." She let Her hands fall on Her knees. "Wars have been fought over these questions, but no answers were produced by all that violence."

Guin poked the roast with her knife, and the juices ran clear. She poked it in a couple more places, with the same result. She hastily transferred it to a tin plate, splashing burning oil onto her hand in the process. She put the burn to her mouth, which gave slight relief. Clawed fingers gently took her wrist and pulled it to the Angel's mouth.

"If you will allow me..."

Guin nodded, and Dusk licked the burn, instantly cooling it while sending little spikes of heat through Guin's body. She pursed Her lips and released a glob of spit onto it, which numbed the area around it. "That should help the process."

Guin wanted to ask how the Angel's saliva could cure her wounds and relieve Ynis' infection, how Her language worked, what She'd tell Her friends and family when She got back. How She'd mourn Her children who didn't make it—maybe even the ones Guin herself had killed.

"Thank you," was all she said as she cut the oily meat off the bones. They ate in relative silence. Guin snuck looks at Dusk eating; She sliced off strips of meat with Her claws and retrieved them with Her long tongue, tearing the meat with Her fangs and chewing thoughtfully. Cliff hog was low on Guin's list of culinary delicacies; even lower without salt, but the taste of freshly roasted meat after days of nothing but hardcakes was better than the finest steak on a feast day.

When Dusk had finished and rinsed Her hands in the pool, She returned to the dwindling fire, whose warmth was superfluous now that the sun was rising. She uttered a few cooing syllables to the geller, who responded in kind, gnawing the last shred of meat from the bones.

"I must leave soon." Dusk's face was wistful, but Her eyes shone with a spark of joy. "I would remain with you if I could. We have...much to learn from each other." Her eyes twinkled as She said this, sending a series of blush-worthy images through Guin's mind. "And while I cannot stay, I can offer you a...gift, if you will accept it. I believe your religion calls them wishes."

Guin's heart leapt, then curled in on itself at the word. The Grey Angel was said to be able to grant wishes like wisdom, curing diseases, or long life. Tradition among Angelites was to keep three heart's desires at the ready, which might change over time: one physical attribute, one virtue, and one personal trait, none of which were ever to be spoken aloud. Some spoke of a fourth, something forbidden; there was some question as to how much morality should be taken into account in the Fourth Desire.

"You may ask for anything you want, and if it is within my power, I will grant it." Dusk glanced from Guin to Ynis and back again. "My abilities may seem miraculous, but I assure you, I can only grant you things your body and mind are already capable of. I can unlock your true potential, as it were."

"So, it's true," Ynis whispered, turning to Guin. "About the Angel granting wishes."

Guin nodded, thinking of the tales of those who'd disappeared and come back changed. "There are stories many take to be true." A woman had come to speak at her church, claiming to be a hundred and twelve years old, though she looked sixty at most. A hermit near the coast of

Irruin was said to have gained the ability to communicate with birds. A farmer could predict weather a week ahead of time. Guin only half-believed the stories. "I've never seen proof."

"And now you shall." Dusk opened Her arms, fanning Her wings out so the sun shone through the tips, gilding Her. "Tell me, Guin; what is your heart's desire? What would you most like to change about yourself?"

Guin grew dizzy as her carefully memorized and pre-pared wishes fluttered through her head, each seeming more trivial than the last. Eyes that never weakened with time, so she would always see the world clearly. Patience in the face of life's many indignities. The memory of her sister, who'd died of wolfpox when Guin was only three. Her cheeks burned as her Fourth Desire covered them all like smoke from a forest fire.

She'd never put it into words as she had the others, but it had been lingering in her heart for some time now. It remained hazy, indistinct, refusing to be named. To say it out loud, if it were beyond the Angel's abilities, would mean facing the fear she'd been fighting for years.

That she was not worthy.

She'd found relief in a few small changes, but to take the final step off the cliff...Guin had never felt confident in her wings. Dusk's gentle fingertips lifted her chin. When Guin met Her eyes, she saw calm depths of gentle certainty. She lifted Her eyebrows, and Guin's mouth opened, spilling out words that made no sense as she spoke them.

"I wish to be a woman."

The Angel blinked. Her smile widened, showing Her pretty fangs. "You already are."

Guin covered her mouth and nose as she sobbed. *She.* She'd already begun to think of herself that way, but still...

A gentle hand touched her back. Guin leaned into it, into Ynis. She could do this. She sniffed, wiping her eyes, though she still hadn't stopped crying. "I want to be a woman like her." She turned to Ynis, whose face collapsed as she pulled Guin in for the tightest hug of her life. Guin squeezed back with all her might, draping herself around Ynis' muscled softness, fingers twining in her braids, the two of them both wetting each other's cheeks with their tears.

"Sweetie, all you have to do is ask," Ynis murmured in her ear as their warm, tear-dampened embrace loosened. Ynis pushed her to arm's length. "I'd be your patron. You *know* I would."

"I know, it's just..." Guin broke down again, falling against Ynis' chest. She'd never dared to dream of transitioning, even just with philters. It was too late, anyway; her body had grown into what it was going to be. Her face would never look like a woman's. The thought of looking for a patron had never occurred to her, and the idea of Ynis—her mena—being her patron was beyond imagining. "I just didn't feel like...I never thought I was ready."

"If you're ready now, I can help you start down that path, if I understand you correctly." Dusk spoke gently, without pushing.

Guin shook her head to clear it, but she could not shake her dizziness at the Angel's words. "How?"

"I can...encourage your body to feminize—grow breasts, alter your fat distribution, change your voice somewhat. You might lose some strength in the process, but that could be offset with exercise. Like Ynis has done with your science, if I am not mistaken?"

"You are not," Ynis said proudly. "Though I think there's a little magic involved in the Shaping."

Dusk blinked, smiling gently. "See it as science or magic, as you prefer. I can do the same for you, though it will take time. The Shaping is another matter entirely, which—"

"I don't..." Guin often hated her cock, and she *always* hated her testicles, but the Angel had seen her as a woman even with them, and Ynis had as well. And they might come in handy someday, if she ever wanted to have children. She glanced at Ynis, wondering if she'd want children, assuming they could find a surrogate. It must have been hard for her, knowing she couldn't—Guin snapped back to the moment as Ynis cocked her head, staring at Guin curiously. "I'll keep my bits for now," she said to the ground.

"I was not suggesting you do otherwise. I merely wanted to be sure what you were asking for. I can teach your body to alter itself, to feminize you in external ways. You should remain fertile, though your chances of engendering children may drop, especially over time."

"We have ways of mitigating that in our world," Ynis said. Was she blushing as well? Guin recalled Ynis' face as she spoke with the children in the courtyard before their expedition. She would make an incredible mother, but being Shaped didn't grant that gift, as far as Guin knew.

"Very well then. If this is truly your wish, we can start right away."

"How?" Guin asked, head spinning with anticipation. She'd thought about this in secret for so long, hiding it almost from herself even, but it had never seemed real. She'd never felt worthy, but now—

"With a kiss." Dusk closed Her eyes, and Her cheeks puffed in and out as if She were generating spit. She opened Her eyes, nodded gently, and pursed Her lips. Guin advanced slowly, noticing a spot of blood at the corner of Her mouth. Was this really happening? Was she ready? Was she *worthy*? The Angel had called her a woman, and Ynis hadn't taken long to adapt, but—

The kiss was wet and bloody; Guin gagged for a moment, then swallowed, suddenly thirsty for more. She sucked hard on Dusk's lips and tongue, greedily drinking down every drop of Her copper, seaweed, and honey taste. Dusk slowed the kiss, then pulled back and touched Her downy forehead to Guin's featherless one.

"Open your mind," the Angel whispered. Her hands clasped the back of Guin's neck as Her tail wrapped gently around her waist. *"Lower your barriers."* Dusk's mind-voice was echoey at first, then rang clearer as Guin relaxed in Her control. *"Your body already knows what to do. I am just going to give it a little push."* Her wings unfurled, then wrapped Guin in a cocoon of dark comfort.

Warmth grew in Guin's mind like the heat from an unseen fireplace. It spread throughout her head, down through her chest, and beyond, leaving tingles in its wake. Heat grew in two spots in her chest, just below her ribcage, and in her testicles, which twinged uncomfortably, as in the wake of a deep orgasm. Guin's fingers tightened around Her waist as a floating sensation crept up her body, spiraling through her chest and into her head, which seemed to open to the sky.

The world dissolved, then reappeared in a softer, almost pastel palette. She was flying now, carried in the Angel's clawed hands, swaddled like a baby. It couldn't be real, but it felt so perfect. They soared over the mountaintops and into the sky, watching the world grow smaller and more insignificant, then vanish in the fluffy whiteness of the clouds. They hovered; Dusk no longer beat Her wings but held Guin in them somehow.

"Remember this place," Her mind-voice said. *"The sky is your home now. You are earthbound no longer."* Guin watched the clouds billow slowly around her, enclosing her in a cushion of bliss. *"When your feet return to the ground, when the filth and hate of the world get to be too much, never forget: You are an Angel now."*

"I'm an Angel now," Guin repeated, the words light as feathers drifting in gentle winds. *"The sky is my home."* They floated for a time, weightless and free, Guin warm and secure in the Angel's wings. At last, they began to sink. Dusk put Her claws around Guin again, somehow grasping her entire body as if she were a sparrow, and unfurled Her resplendent grey wings again.

"We must go now." Her mind-voice was thick with regret. *"I must see to Ynis' desires. But you can come back here any time, in the same way you found me before. You are an Angel now."*

With a lurch, they dropped out of the clouds, freefalling for a moment before Dusk pointed Her wings back, and they hurtled toward the ground with impossible speed. Guin smiled as the wind whipped past her face; no harm could come to her while in Her arms. As the ground finally approached, Dusk slowed them with a few powerful flaps. Guin saw herself and the Angel below, connected at the forehead, with Ynis looking on solemnly. She landed back in her body with a gentle pop, swaying for a moment, held up by Dusk's tail.

Her skin tingled, as if she'd smoked horseroot flower. The heat in her chest and testicles remained, though it was a gentle burn now. She touched her face, her chest, her hips; all were as they'd been before.

"It will take some time," Dusk said, laying a hand on her cheek. "Your body has received the message and will respond before you know it."

"Thank you," Guin said in a small voice.

"It is the very least I could do, after the gift you gave me. Thank *you*." Dusk cupped the back of her head as Her tail released. "And you," She said, turning to Ynis. "What is it your heart most desires?"

Thirteen

Ynis stared into Dusk's dark eyes, her mind blank with panic. Her heart's desire had already been fulfilled twice over. The woman she realized she'd come to love had found herself, and the Angel she'd never believed in had found her. What more could she ask for?

"There's nothing I want that I don't already have." The words rang false as she spoke them. Ynis steeled herself against the surge of sorrow welling up inside.

"Nothing?" Dusk's voice was soft, probing. She knew.

"Nothing you could give me, anyway."

Dusk looked deep into her eyes, peeling away the layers and unraveling her certainty. There *was* something she'd always wanted, but not even the Angel could give her that gift. "If you do not ask, you will never know," She said in a low, almost motherly voice that touched Ynis in a place she'd forgotten existed.

Ynis' face and nose flushed with the onset of tears, which it was pointless to stop. The only question was whether she'd muster the courage to say the words. She took in a shallow breath and let out a shuddering sigh.

"I doubt this is in your power, but…" She glanced at Guin through her tear-streaked vision, keeping a sob at bay with great effort. "My body has been Shaped, but on the inside, I lack…that is, I cannot…" Dusk nodded, saying nothing. "I have always wished I could become a mother."

Dusk frowned, then placed Her hands on the sides of Ynis' head and leaned in to touch foreheads with her. Ynis closed her eyes as a blankness spread in her mind, like mist covering the surface of a lake, erasing all thought. It was almost comforting, being this empty, this not-in-control. She could get used to this.

"…may be complicated, as our reproductive systems are somewhat different," Dusk was saying as Ynis came to her senses. "I might be breaking the law regarding repro-ductive intervention in my world, but we're not in my world, are we? At any rate, I *should* be able to instigate the process."

"Do it," Ynis breathed, never so sure of anything in her life.

Dusk frowned again, looking Ynis up and down. "It will be a long process, and a painful one."

"I don't care." Her tears flowed freely now, but a tide of joy was overtaking her long-guarded sorrow.

"Your body will have to reconfigure itself from within. As new tissue grows, new organs form, others must adapt. The pain may be crippling. You may be unable to fight, unable to work, unable to…" She glanced at Guin, then back at Ynis, casting Her eyes down. "You may be unable to do many of the things you enjoy for the better part of a year."

"Sounds like the price all pay to become mothers." Ynis glanced at Guin, who nodded through tears just as thick as her own. She turned back at the Angel. "Do it."

Dusk blinked and sighed, Her face looking suddenly exhausted, as if the weight of this world was dragging Her down. When She smiled again, the clouds lifted from Her face, and from Ynis' heart. She closed Her hands around Ynis' head and pressed foreheads again. "Though the horizon be far and the trials many, we endure."

The silence that followed was absolute. Ynis felt her mind opening, the grey mist of the Angel's presence billowing in like ink spilled into water. An ache grew in her chest, then flowed down and settled in her belly, like the heaviness the day before her cycles. Something was churning deep within, something needy, *hungry*. Something whose only source of food was her own flesh. The ache grew to fill her entire lower half before dulling slightly, with two hot spots, one on either side of her stomach. As the Angel released, Ynis doubled over and vomited, splashing her breakfast over her boots as Dusk skipped nimbly back.

"The first of many, I assure you." Dusk put a hand on her shoulder as Ynis stood slowly, wiping her mouth with a handkerchief. "A badge of honor." She stepped back again as Ynis put a hand to her mouth, then turned to the side and threw up again.

"I'll wear it with pride," she said, mouth still leaking into the puddle on the ground.

in somber silence; Dusk kissed Ynis with finality, lingering in the moment their lips pulled apart before pulling back and pursing Her lips. "I do not know if we shall meet again." She touched them both on the shoulder, then put a hand on the head of the geller, who squatted next to Her. "When I return to this world, I will look for you in the quiet hours of the night."

"And you will find us," Guin said in a trembling voice.

Dusk blinked softly. "Farewell." She uttered a brief syllable to the geller, who stood, looking each of them in the eyes, and blinked at them in turn as Dusk had done. At another fluid word from the Angel, the geller dropped to all fours, turned, and trotted off on the little path around the pond.

Dusk turned slowly, eyes shifting to the ground. She walked, not down the path toward the geller, but to the pond's edge. The geller had stopped, never leaving Her sight, and stared back at Her with curious eyes. She stooped to the ground and picked up a pebble. She hefted it in Her hand a few times, then placed it carefully atop Ynis and Guin's pebbles. She stood staring at the pond for a moment, then without a glance back, the Grey Angel turned and followed the geller into the trees.

A cold drizzle fell as they descended, eventually soaking them to the skin. It made travel slow, which was a good thing. Dusk had healed their more obvious wounds, but the stress and fatigue of the journey had taken its toll. To make matters worse, Ynis had the worst cramps she'd ever had in her life. It wasn't time for her cycle, but something was happening inside her. The horizon would be far, as Dusk had said, and the trials many. The thought lifted her spirit as they made their way down along the creek, following game trails where they could see them and tramping their way down when they could not.

Guin seemed to be in a similar headspace. They talked little while the rain fell, but it died down to mist as they set up camp, loosening their tongues.

"Cramps?" Guin asked with a gentle blink.

Ynis nodded. "That obvious?"

Guin sniffed a little laugh through her nose. "I guess I have that to look forward to as well, if…" She looked down, as if hoping to see breasts already after just a few hours.

"You never know. Not all Chosen women get them. Though if—" Ynis stopped herself. Not everyone wanted to be Shaped. Guin had said she'd keep her bits for now, and in any case, it wasn't her business. "Never mind," she said with a little smile. "I didn't—"

"You're fine," Guin said softly. "I don't think so, I just…" She picked at her nails, then looked up, sort of squinting in the growing dusk. "I guess there's more than one way to be a mother." She shook her head quickly, eyes darting back down to her hands. "Not that, I mean—"

"No, I get it!" Ynis said hurriedly as she studied her own fingernails. Her heart thudded in her chest, and were those tears threatening to form? "There are always compromises." She'd never regretted being Shaped. It was the best thing that had ever happened to her. That and the injections that had remade the rest of her body. But knowing that she was giving up the chance to ever have children of her own had been a bitter pill to swallow. She almost didn't believe it was real—could a being, even one from another world, really do *that*? Dual twinges on either side of her belly drove home exactly how real this was.

"How about you?" Guin asked, dusting her hands off now that the tarp was stretched tight between two saplings. "How are you feeling about...all of this?"

Ynis opened her mouth, then closed it. Her mind had been strangely empty most of the day. She'd thought about the immediate, practical things—the pain, the need to rest, who would lead the squadron when she was unable to, how they would handle the geller going forward—but she hadn't asked herself how she *felt* about it all.

"I don't know, I guess it hasn't really sunk in yet. Like, I'll believe it when I see it. I'll believe it when I bleed. Maybe then I'll know how to feel."

Ynis didn't notice she was crying until Guin wrapped her in a big, soft hug.

That night, they lay snuggled together against the damp chill, having abandoned their attempts to keep a fire going. Ynis was the big spoon, wrapping Guin up tight. Whatever Ynis was about to go through, Guin's journey would be harder. Guin had fought it for so long, fought *herself* for so long; as her body changed, that battle would drag on for years, if not a lifetime. Even in the Queendom, with all the support of her family, her community, and the crown, Ynis had daily doubts that might not go away even if the Angel's miracle turned out to be entirely real. She kissed Guin's ear. Guin snuggled closer, humming contentedly in her sleep.

FOURTEEN

As they were descending the next day, Guin saw a falcon circle overhead, then swoop down and land on Ynis' outstretched arm. "Whoa there," Ynis said as the bird spread its wings wide, then settled them down its back. She shucked one glove and removed the little scroll from its tube. Guin sidled closer to get a look, and Ynis showed her the scroll with a sigh.

Rescue en route. Stay put.

Ynis fished out a pencil and pressed the paper against a boulder.

We are safe. Descending now. Meet on Bottoms Road.

She rolled the scroll back up and slid it into the tube. The falcon spread its wings once again and took off without a sound. "I hope they bring something to eat besides hardcakes," Ynis said as they watched the bird flap off.

"I could go for some gormin shank with crispy earthroot right about now." Guin's mouth watered at the thought, and her stomach twisted itself further into a knot. They still had a full day's hike to get to the road, and they were out of food entirely.

"I could eat a barrel of pickles," Ynis said. "And a loaf of crusty dark bread." She sighed and began walking again. "We'd better get moving if we want off this mountain by nightfall."

They reached the road a little before dark and camped in the same spot they'd used on their way up, since they'd already done the work of clearing it.

"I'll take first watch," Guin said, eyeing the dark forest. They hadn't seen any more signs of geller on the way down, but tired as they were, this wasn't the time to let down their guard.

"Did I ever tell you how amazing you are?" Ynis unrolled her sleep pocket, which had crusty stains from their night with the Angel, like Guin's.

"You too," Guin managed, unsure how to navigate the unfamiliar terrain of their new relationship, if that's what this was. Or was it? Surely not. Ynis was just being protective because of Guin's newly hatched status. It was Dusk's presence that had made her kiss Guin. Whatever had happened on the mountain, Guin had no expectation that it would continue.

"No, I mean it," Ynis said, turning around so Guin could undo the straps on her armor. "I've always known I could trust you. That's why I chose you for this mission." She turned around to face Guin, who undid the final straps and removed her shoulder guards and breastplate. "But I've come to see a new side of you. Or rather, a side of you I'd been ignoring up til now."

"What side is that?" Guin averted her eyes with great difficulty as she helped pull the mail shirt over Ynis' head. Ynis removed her greaves and slipped out of her mail pants. Ynis laid them with the rest of her armor and stepped toward Guin, little more than the outline of a woman in the growing darkness.

"You're selfless and kind, unflinching in the face of danger." Her hands gripped Guin's forearms as she pulled closer. Heat radiated from her body through her underclothes. Guin was thankful for the darkness to hide the evidence of her desire rising up against her will. "And you were so tender with the Angel...and with me." Her breath was hot on Guin's face now, hands sliding up Guin's arms to frame her shoulders, the tips of her soft breasts pressing against Guin's chest.

The kiss turned Guin's heart inside out. Ynis' lips were soft and smooth; the faint aftertaste of her lipstick lingered even as the kiss deepened. Ynis held Guin firmly, one hand sliding up the back of her neck as their tongues tangled, flooding Guin's chest with euphoric warmth. She'd been kissed by plenty of women in her life, but never in a way that made her feel like a woman herself. The way Ynis handled her, the strength of her grip, the heedless mashing of her lips against Guin's—she'd never felt wanted like this before. Her hands found Ynis' hips, hard muscles beneath her rounded shape, and held on gently as they lingered in the kiss, then finally separated, breath husky and lips tingling.

"When we get back, and fed, and bathed, and slept..." Ynis traced a line across Guin's brow and down along her cheek. "I'd like to pick up where we just left off."

Watch was long, hungry, and cold, but the memory of that kiss combined with Ynis' promise kept Guin occupied during the still watches of the night.

The medic unit met them near Feyan's Bog with water, fresh fruit, and to their utter surprise and delight, a whole roast prairie hen with earthroots that were still almost crispy.

"Queen's orders," the doctor said as they fell upon the food like famished wolves.

"Long live the Queen, and long live the Queendom," Ynis said through a mouthful of chicken. Guin held up a fry, then ate it to honor the Queen and the Queendom.

"Long live anyone with a constitution like yours, Mena. I can't believe this didn't kill you." The doctor dabbed ointment on the wound, though Ynis was still eating.

"Kind of you to be so frank, doctor."

"I prefer not to lie to my patients, and I expect the same in return." She laid a fresh bandage on the wound, pressing the sticky edges against her skin. "This wound looks like it happened two weeks ago. It's almost healed, and there's no infection whatsoever." She eyed Ynis seriously, then turned her attention toward Guin. "Something wrong with your back?"

"A rock fell on it. It's pretty sore, but..." She stretched her arms out, rotating side to side, with little pain. She wondered if the Angel had healed her back too somehow. "My armor and padding took the worst of it."

"We'll have a look on the way back. Finish your food and we'll get you in the wagon and on your way home."

She nodded from Guin to Ynis, then turned and began conferring with the driver.

They sat alone on the folded-out back of the ambulance, which Guin noted had leaf and coil suspension. She had a habit of studying carriages, ever since she was a child and rode in her first Seelie. It was like riding on a cloud of air.

"Should be a comfy ride," Ynis said, stuffing another fry into her mouth. "Leaf and coil suspension. That's what the—"

"Queen's carriage uses, yes! I read that the new steel-tempering process at Maidenhead Forge allows for a unique combination of flexibility and strength. They won't say what they've added, but my money's on..." Guin pattered on for a while before realizing what she was doing. Ynis was studying her, still chewing, eyes alight with something Guin had never dared hope to see. "Anyway, I don't want to bore you with carriage talk. It's just a little...hobby of mine, I guess you could say."

"It's funny you should mention it, because my uncle has an old Seelie dry-rotting in his barn. I was thinking of trying to fix it up."

"Is that the ten-spoke or the twelve-spoke?"

Ynis put a hand to her chin for a moment. "You know, I'm not sure. It's got a leathered top, or *had*; it's torn to shit now."

"Oh! That's the twelve-spoke. It has—"

"Pull-out storage front and back," the driver said, pulling on her gloves as she approached. "You'll pay extra in tariffs for parts from the Kingdom, but for a twelve-spoke Seelie? It's worth it." She glanced up at the horizon, as if studying the sky, though there were no clouds to be seen. "*If* the frame's not too rusted." She wagged her finger at Ynis, then let it drop, shrugging apologetically. "Sorry, I—"

"Can tell me all about it when we stop for the night."

"I—well, that is, technically, I'm not supposed to—" She was flustered by Ynis; most women were. A twinge in Guin's chest told her she was actually *jealous*.

"Then it's settled. The good doctor will tend to our health on the way, and when we arrive, you can tell us everything we need to know if we're to take on this project." Guin fielded Ynis' smile with as much grace as she could, given her use of the words *us* and *we*. Did that mean... "That is, if you're game, I thought it might be—but I didn't—"

"You're fine!" Guin tried to blink away her embarrassment. "I mean, yes, I'd love to restore a twelve-spoke Seelie with you."

Ynis bit her lip, eyes crackling with something wicked and good. "That might just be the hottest thing anyone's ever said to me."

Their landing in the castle was smooth, with plenty of food and rest before they gave their report. They'd agreed to make no mention of the Angel and give the pond as the place they'd burned the geller's body. There weren't enough Haemene to go around as it was; they weren't going to send another unit just to corroborate their story. Even if they did, the cliff hog's remains might fool them.

The mission interview went fine after all. The purview officer stamped the file closed, and they were soon on their own again, with ten days of mandated rest and recovery. "Avoid strenuous engagements for the first five days," her doctor had said rather pointedly. "Your body needs rest to be at its best." Guin nodded, thinking of all the extra work her body was doing. She could feel it, little hot spots just below her belly, but more than that, in the way people treated her, even before she told them.

"There's something else, I—" Guin took a breath before continuing. She'd practiced with Ynis, who'd been so sweet about everything, never making her feel stupid for asking the littlest questions. She'd need medical care as her body changed, someone who understood how things worked. There were tests they could do, something about blood levels, she wasn't quite sure.

"I'd like a consult at a flower house. I'm choosing to live as the woman I am. The woman I've become." She bit her lip and didn't cry. She wasn't going to cry over every little thing. She could be strong. The doctor's quick, warm smile told her this might not have been the big surprise she'd imagined. Everyone had been quite lovely about it, in fact.

"Of course, that's wonderful! Are you thinking Bleny or Quinn? Or maybe Awning? Or the university clinic can often get you in faster, so long as you agree to let doctoral students observe your appointment."

"I don't know, I...a friend of mine went to Awning. She seemed to like it. I think I'll go there."

"Excellent! I'll get a certificate of health ready." She pulled out a booklet of printed forms and scribbled wildly on one of them, then tore it out carefully. "I'd love to see you in three months, once you've met with your doctor, in case there's anything else I should know."

"Thank you, I—thank you."

"My pleasure." The doctor held out her knuckles, and Guin tapped them with her own. Not everyone had adapted the Queendom's edict discouraging handshakes, so it was nice to see, especially from a medical professional.

Soon she was out the door, a free woman with nothing but time on her hands. She sent off a gram to Awning when she got back and received a response the next morning. She had an intake appointment in two weeks. She'd prepared a story about a Finding ceremony, a ritual from the tundra to the north, said to unlock a person's true identity, sometimes even helping people change sex over time. It was plausible enough, and from what she'd heard, the general philosophy in flower houses was not to ask unnecessary questions.

She was lucky to live in the Queendom.

She lay awake each night, mind open, waiting for the Grey Angel. It felt strange, now that she'd met Dusk. The chances of being visited again were infinitesimal, and did she really want to meet another Angel? She used her nightly ritual as a place to live with the memory of Her, of the night they'd shared together, of the gift She'd given. Guin's nipples itched suddenly against her thin nightshirt; they were sensitive since they'd started growing, which made it hard to focus sometimes. She shook her head and pictured Dusk's face, the dark heat of Her eyes, and everything else fell away.

Guin spoke with Her sometimes, in the cozy little corner of the clouds where the Angel had flown her in her vision.

"Where are you now?" she'd ask. "What are you doing?"

"In the kitchen, checking my pies," She'd respond, or "Up to my neck in paperwork."

It was amusing, trying to imagine Dusk living a normal life, filling out forms, burning Her thumb on a hot pan. And the geller, the one they'd met, would her wings have started growing? Or maybe she had grown and flown off on her own by now. Dusk had said time was inconsistent between worlds. Maybe the next Angel she met would be her own child. Maybe the next geller would be.

Ynis had had a frank talk with the General, who'd gotten her an audience with the Queen to convince her to stop the geller hunts immediately. Guin wished she could have been there to see the Queen's face as Ynis told her the truth about their visit from the Angel. 'The *whole* truth,' Ynis said with a wicked glint in her eye. The Queen had agreed immediately and commissioned Ynis to help the

General come up with an alternate plan. Ynis had been offered a lieutenantship, which she'd accepted. It would entail more administrative duties, a benefit on her bad pain days, which were increasingly frequent.

Guin blinked to clear her mind. The Angel wasn't going to visit her while she was worried about the events of the world. She summoned, not Dusk's face, but the old face she used to use, before she'd met the real thing. This Angel was a little sad, or maybe disappointed, with just a soupçon of hope in Her eyes, like in the old books. Guin could understand the sadness, the disappointment. The very humans She needed for procreation also killed Her children. It was hardly unusual; most species didn't expect half of their offspring to survive to adulthood. It must have been hard to hold onto that glimmer of hope in the face of such odds.

Guin shook her head and uncrossed her arms. No Angel was going to visit her tonight, as distracted as she was. She leaned over for a sip of water before going to sleep and noticed a shape across the dark room. A woman stood in the open doorway, face bathed in shadow, eyes glinting in the dark. She beckoned with a curled finger, then stood still as a statue. Guin slipped out of bed, careful not to shake the squeaky frame, and padded across the cold floor on bare feet. The figure backed out into the hall as she approached, then closed the door silently behind her. She turned, stripes of grey from a windowpane illuminating her dark features.

Ynis said nothing as she took Guin by the hand and led her down the hallway.

The Angel had come for her after all.

FIFTEEN

Ynis' heart fluttered as if she'd run a great distance, though all she'd done was lead Guin up a flight of stairs and down the hall to her room. She'd shut the door behind her and leaned against it, smiling like a kid sneaking cookies from the cupboard in the middle of the night.

"What's going on?" Guin asked in a faint whisper.

Ynis plucked up her courage, bit her lip in what she hoped was a provocative way, and pulled her nightshirt over her head. Guin's slack-jawed attention told her she'd hit her mark. She shimmied out of her underpants, shaking off the fear of her body's imperfections. Were her hips too straight? Was her jaw too strong? Were her shoulders too broad? No matter how many women threw themselves at her, there was always a little bitch-ass voice in her ear snarking at her flaws.

Guin's rising erection as Ynis approached with slow, silent steps shut the voice down. Guin maintained eye contact, though Ynis could feel the strain as Guin strove not to stare at her breasts. She stopped and cupped them in her hands, squeezing her nipples a little; that got Guin's eyes to stray, if only for an instant.

"It's okay to look at my tits." Ynis let them fall, stepping closer. "It's okay to want me." She closed the scant distance between them, lifting a hand to trace the backs of her fingers down Guin's freshly shaven cheek. "You do, don't you?"

"Yes," Guin breathed without hesitation, standing rigid as a coatrack. Ynis leaned in to kiss her, soft and brief, making sure her breasts pressed against Guin's chest.

"Take off your clothes," she whispered in Guin's ear, then stepped back and crossed her arms over her chest. She wasn't sure what she was doing; she didn't usually go in for theatrics, but Guin was so stiff, so hesitant. Ynis needed to see her façade crack.

Guin's expression took on a desperate, almost pitiful quality as she tugged her nightshirt over her head and tossed it onto the bed. It was a flimsy thing in gossamer weave, given to her at her first visit to the clinic. Ynis remembered how sensitive her nipples had been at first. She was going to have to be gentle with Guin. Guin looked down as she bent awkwardly to pull down her pants, as if to hide her cock, though when she stood back up again, there was no mistaking her desire. The only question was, what would make Guin feel desired herself? Not all newly hatched women were comfortable with their equipment, but Guin had said she wanted to keep it, so who knew?

"May I touch you?" Ynis asked, uncrossing her arms again, flushing as Guin's eyes fell to her breasts, then down between her legs before flickering back up to meet hers.

Guin nodded. "Yes," she croaked, eyes weak and wet.

Ynis stepped closer, running her fingers up Guin's sculpted arms, over her muscled shoulders, and down the broad expanse of her chest, which felt like it had been recently waxed. She feathered her fingertips lightly over the tops of Guin's pebbled areolas, then circled slowly, attentive to Guin's little gasps.

She kissed Guin in the midst of one such gasp, taking advantage of the opening to move in with her tongue. Guin put her hands on Ynis' forearms and kissed her back softly, letting Ynis take the lead. Guin's lips froze as Ynis gently pinched her nipples, then released, and again, and again. Guin's breath came in ragged huffs as Ynis kissed her way down her chin and neck, across her chest, kissing little circles around each nipple. One hand slid around to grip Guin's firm behind while the fingers of the other grazed her cock as a test. Guin let out a little whine, which Ynis took for a positive sign. She worked Guin over with gentle fingertips, ever kissing around and around, letting her lips get closer and closer.

When Ynis flicked her tongue over Guin's nipple, Guin gave a brief whine, then clamped her hand over her own mouth.

"Such a sensitive girl," Ynis said between licks. "So eager." She licked a little harder now, giving more pressure with her fingers, feeling Guin throb, hot and ready, beneath her touch. "When I do this," she said as she licked Guin again and again, "what does it make you want to do to me?" She maintained eye contact as she sucked Guin's nipple into her mouth, watching her face melt into a mask of pained delight. She released with an audible *pop*, then stood and locked eyes with Guin, daring her to make the next move.

Guin's eyes hardened in the way they sometimes did before battle, gleaming like bright stars in the darkness. She gripped Ynis by the shoulders with surprising force and walked her the two steps back to the edge of her little bed. Heat flared in Ynis' belly as Guin pushed her shoulders down. She ran her strong hands across Ynis' breasts, calloused fingers dragging over her nipples. Guin kissed her way down Ynis' body with rough abandon. Her hands gripped ever lower and pulled Ynis to the edge of the bed. Guin knelt before her, looking Ynis up and down like a cut of rare steak, setting Ynis' heart racing and her juices flowing.

Guin started with the tenderest kisses on her inner thigh. Her lips were so soft, her kisses so delicate, her warm breath on Ynis' skin so enticing. She kissed her way in, close, so close, but her lips moved up and over, then down the other side and down the crease of her thigh, licking now, as Ynis sighed with desperation. Guin's finger teased the bottom of her entrance, tugging her open, slipping just inside, but not far enough, not nearly far enough. By the time Guin's tongue had finished painting every part of her except the ones that counted, Ynis was dripping, melting, panting.

Guin's finger slid in as she licked her way up Ynis' cunt with torturous patience. She sent Ynis to the very edge as her tongue brushed against her clit, lingering, circling, too light to make her come but so close, so very close. After a few more slow passes, Guin began to feast in earnest, shooting Ynis up and beyond her first climax with a relentless assault of fingertips and tongue. She slowed then, kissing gently around Ynis' folds, then up her stomach, one finger still resting halfway in as her other hand slid up to grab a handful of breast. As Guin hovered above her,

Ynis tried to sneak a hand down to touch Guin's cock. She quickly found herself with both hands pinned against the wall, mouth filled with her own taste as Guin plundered her.

Ynis had meant to direct Guin, to show her how she liked to be pleased, what she wanted, but Guin had other plans—plans that included ravishing Ynis with every part of her except her cock over and over and over. Ynis chased her own pleasure from orgasm to exploding orgasm, writhing beneath Guin's touch, her body afire with a deeper burn than she'd ever known possible.

In her few moments of coherent thought between climaxes, Ynis wondered if what was happening inside her, what the Angel had done to her, was making her—she let out a beastly groan, quickly stifled by Guin's firm hand over her mouth, as Guin tongue-fucked her into oblivion. Her body seemed to levitate off the bed. Guin rose with her, gripping her buttocks tight with one hand, keeping the other clamped over her mouth, all while somehow driving her into the aether of ecstasy.

Ynis' breath grew short, then nonexistent. Red splotches formed in her vision. Silence rang in her ears as she crashed to the bed, legs still shaking, arms flopping like wet noodles. Guin wrapped herself around Ynis, kissing her belly and chest, chin and cheek. Once Ynis finally gasped a huge breath in and let it out, Guin's lips found hers, slick and heady with her scent, her taste. Guin collapsed to the side, breath hot in her ear, body slumped over hers as little tremors ran through her, echoes of pleasure trickling out of her little by little. Neither spoke as their bodies recovered, glued together with sweat and cum, the air perfumed with their lovemaking.

"My Angel," Ynis breathed into the darkness, stroking Guin's sweat-matted hair. Guin hummed in response, hand secure on her hip, lips pressed into her shoulder.

"I wonder what She's doing now," Guin murmured after a time.

"Making love and thinking of us, I hope." Ynis pictured Dusk, wings spread, pinning Her mate down—or were there more than one of them? She'd said *many* when asked whom She loved. Maybe Angels weren't meant to have just one lover. Maybe they were meant to share themselves with the world. "Do you think She'll come back?" she asked.

Guin remained silent for a long moment.

"When we need Her most, our Angel will come for us."

Ynis tried to stifle her giggle at the double entendre, given the solemnity of Guin's voice. She let it all out when Guin snorted, both of them shaking with laughter they didn't even try to contain. Let the other soldiers hear them.

Let them talk. This was the Queendom, after all. It was right there in the First Principles:

Let kindness and light ever lift you up and bring forth in your heart a garden of joy.

Epilogue

Guin took Ynis' cloak and pulled out a chair for her to slump into.

"Thanks, Angel." Ynis had taken to calling her that, and Guin didn't hate it.

"Cup of tea?" Guin asked, already pouring it.

"Gods, yes." Ynis accepted the cup and a quick peck on the lips. Her smile was genuine but quickly faded into a grimace of pain. Guin didn't ask how Council was; Ynis would share when she was ready, and until then, such problems had no place in their lives. "How're the new recruits?"

Guin snorted. "If they were any greener, they'd be growing on trees." She smiled. Two of the newbies on her squad seemed all right. The third was a skittish person with no business going out on patrol, but ze was the General's child, so she'd have to find a use for zer.

"You'll need to season them up quick." Ynis winced as she took what must have been a too-large sip of hot tea.

"More geller?" There hadn't been any spotted for months. It could be years before they came back, or it could be tomorrow.

Ynis shook her head, jaw set in the way she had when her insides were bothering her. "Spies from the Kingdom. In the northern ridges."

Guin cocked her head. "What are they spying on up there?" It was two weeks' ride to nowhere, with the last week through mostly uninhabited scrubland.

"If the General knows, she's not telling. But we were told to double our numbers by year's end." She clenched her fist and let it rest on the table. "It's gonna be a shit-show." She took another sip of tea, face etched in a pained frown.

Guin sat across the little table from her and took her hand. "Anything I can do to help you feel better?"

Ynis shook her head, squeezing Guin's hand. "Doctor says things are coming along nicely. All the parts have formed, but they have some growing to do yet. A few more months..." A tear slid down her cheek, but she wiped it off before it could go far. "I'll be fine. I just need to rest, is all."

Guin caressed her hand with her thumb. "And when exactly are you going to do that?"

Ynis blinked, her stoic smile slipping for a moment. "Just as soon as we hit our recruiting numbers."

Guin pulled Ynis' hand closer, interlacing fingers with her. "If you don't rest, things might take longer. Things might—" She stopped herself. "You know what the doctor said."

Ynis pulled Guin's hand to her lips and kissed it. "Just a few more days, then I promise, I'll take a whole day off and spend it with you."

"A whole day? You'll get bedsores."

"Oh, I'll get bedsores all right." She kissed her way up Guin's finger, then sucked it into her mouth, one digit at a time, pumping, licking.

"I hate it when you distract me from pointing out your—oh!" Guin gasped as Ynis' hand slid between her legs and held her with a firm grip. Ynis deftly undid Guin's belt and peeled open her pants as she got to her knees before Guin. "Ynis, I don't think in your condit—"

Guin lost the ability to speak, even to think, as Ynis took her deep into her hot, wet mouth with no preamble. What Ynis did to her, the way she touched, it was as if she'd peeled away the man-flesh and found her woman-hood throbbing inside. Guin closed her eyes and clutched her tender budding breasts, imagining Ynis eating her out, each lick, flick, and suck delving deeper, coiling the spring of her pleasure ever tighter. When at last she came, the world disappeared; all sight and sound compressed into a single point of silent darkness before her body exploded with blind ecstasy.

Guin was crying when the darkness faded and the room came back into focus. Ynis smiled up at her, wet-faced and wicked with glee.

"I think we set a new record." She wiped her face with an already cum-slicked hand, looking around for someplace to wipe it. "These pants will need a good wash anyway." She smirked as she wiped her hand on Guin's pants, then gripped her knees to rise up for a quick, salty kiss.

"I'm sorry, gods, I..." Guin couldn't stop the snort that came out as she pulled her hand back from Ynis' hair and found it sticky and wet. Ynis snorted in response, covering her mouth, bumping foreheads with Guin as their bodies rocked with laughter.

"Don't be sorry, Angel." Ynis' face grew serious, running a finger down Guin's cheek. "Your pleasure is my pleasure."

"Mena," Guin murmured, tears welling in her eyes as their lips met and the world dissolved in a haze of feathery grey.

Also By Dani Finn

All books and other links can be found on my Link-tree.

The Maer Cycle (*Hollow Road, The Archive,* and *The Place Below*), a classic fantasy trilogy with LGBTQ characters. It tells the story of the encounter between humans and the legendary hairy humanoids called the Maer and the struggle for the two peoples to reconcile their history and their future.

The Weirdwater Confluence duology (*The Living Waters* and *The Isle of a Thousand Worlds*) are a pair of romantic fantasy books with meditation magic. They are independent of the trilogy, but there are little connections. Both books are sword-free and death-free, in sharp contrast to the Maer Cycle.

Unpainted is a standalone arranged marriage fantasy romance set in the Weirdwater universe, and *The World Within* is a standalone trans sapphic fantasy romance that includes some of the characters from *Unpainted*.

The Time Before: *The Delve, Jagged Shard, Wings so Soft,* and *Cloti's Song,* a group of linked romantic fantasy standalones set 2,000 years before the Maer Cycle. Meant to be read before or after the other books, they tell the story of the fall of the great Maer civilization of old.

Scrublands: A new Switzerland-inspired, western-themed fantasy world. *They of the West* is a novella of friendship and self-discovery about two teens who go chasing after treasure in forbidden canyons.

Short stories: The Winnie and Crela series, beginning with *Barrow Maid,* a lesbian ghoul-necrologist romance; *User Not Found,* a trans lesbian dystopian censorship tale; *Fly by Night,* a trans lesbian butterfly-moth romance; and *The Last Solstice Gift,* a family vignette set in the Time Before, featuring characters from *Wings so Soft* and *Cloti's Song.*

Acknowledgements

Thank you first and foremost to my wife, who gives me life, and my kids, who make me laugh, and my cats, who make me smile.

This book would not exist without the help and encouragement of May Peterson, my mentor and sensitivity editor. She helps me believe that my vision is not only possible; it's inevitable.

Huge thanks to Chris Zable, my editor, who's as good with commas and word choice as she is at making sure the sexual anatomy of beings from other worlds remains consistent throughout the manuscript.

Big shout-out to Allison Ashtear, who drew the gorgeous cover art, and whose comics are amazing and you should definitely read them.

Many thanks to Emma Rowan, who was so generous with her time and talent in drawing the fonts for the cover.

Thanks to my discord crew, including but not limited to May, Tris, Sophia, and Arra, who helped inspire me and cheer me on as I sank into this story.

Thanks to all the trans folks on Bluesky for making it a haven for a late bloomer like me.

And thanks to you, dear reader, for following me on this strange adventure. I hope you join me again sometime soon!